Dr

DRIFT

CARYL LEWIS

PENGUIN BOOKS

TRANSWORLD PUBLISHERS
Penguin Random House, One Embassy Gardens,
8 Viaduct Gardens, London SW11 7BW
www.penguin.co.uk

Transworld is part of the Penguin Random House group of companies
whose addresses can be found at global.penguinrandomhouse.com

Penguin
Random House
UK

First published in Great Britain in 2022 by Doubleday
an imprint of Transworld Publishers
Penguin paperback edition published 2023

A CIP catalogue record for this book
is available from the British Library.

ISBN 9781804990889

Typeset in Granjon by Jouve (UK), Milton Keynes.
Printed and bound in Great Britain by Clays Ltd, Elcograf S.p.A.

The authorized representative in the EEA is Penguin Random House Ireland,
Morrison Chambers, 32 Nassau Street, Dublin D02 YH68.

Penguin Random House is committed to a sustainable
future for our business, our readers and our planet. This book
is made from Forest Stewardship Council® certified paper.

For my mother. Who was right.

Gobaith

'Rwy'n ofni'r distawrwydd sy'n dyfod,
Distawrwydd didostur y sêr;
Fy mhobl na fynnwch ymwared,
'Rwy'n meithrin eich marw'n fy mêr.

Ac eto ni allaf beidio
Â chredu'n fy nghalon ddofn
Fod yr hen fynyddoedd yn amau
Ac yn loetran o gwmpas rhag ofn.

Hope

I fear the silence that's coming,
The merciless silence of stars;
My people who refuse deliverance,
I nurse your death in my bones.

And yet, I cannot but believe,
In the deepest places of my heart,
That the old mountains are undecided,
And linger on to play their part.

Gerallt Lloyd Owen

Strandline ✦ *Traethlin* ✦ *Alkhatu alsaahiliu*

THE COVE HAD ALWAYS called things to it. Her father would blame the jutting headland, saying that it slowed the tide so that it brought forth its offerings. Her mother used to say that it was something much more than that. That the sea would show you what you needed it to, in its own time, and that the only thing you could do was wait. There would be driftwood, of course, bleached white; tangles of fishing nets and constellations of starfish so dense they'd thicken the waters with their numbers. There had been bodies, too, seal-grey and ashen, gently nudged to the sands, the victims of storms and shipping lanes or broken souls who had trusted themselves to the deep. Their pockets would be checked for change, before they were dragged to the dune-swamped church. There they'd be placed in paupers' graves, each wooden cross marked with which tide had brought them in, as if the sea's giving and its taking away made any difference.

Nefyn stood, holding her breath, the dark pools exposed by the slack-water glistening around her, the limpets gasping for the tide. She listened as the sandpipers and plovers, stark in winter plumage, questioned the dawn moon with their cries. She hadn't been able to sleep for weeks, her tiredness making her feel as if she were drowning. She exhaled, her breath billowing into the blue stillness. From here she could see the curve of the coast. The warm glow of lights over the sleeping village a few miles to the south, and to the north, the sharp angles of the military base, unnaturally rigid, magnified somehow by the weight of rain in the sky.

She turned, pulled her coat around her, and walked barefoot along the beach in search of today's offerings. The strandline lay just out of reach of the water, a fragile trail that traced the coast, configured and reconfigured at each tide's turn. An ever-present collection of disparate things brought temporarily together. The glass cabinets in the cottage were full of specimens she had collected over the years, shells and whelks, egg cases and seeds. So now she would only bring home the most remarkable things, knowing she would have to sacrifice a beloved object for its place. Her feet found footholds along the shingle beach, her soles impervious to its grit, having walked this way since she was a girl.

The cove was deep, the steepness of its rise making sound move differently, voices reverberate more, making light linger a little longer. You could not hide anything from the sea; the cove itself was evidence of this. The waves had sought out and worn the softness of the coast away in their merciless quest to expose its hidden shape. Her father had dared build a boatshed at the foot of the cliffs and spent his life launching his boat from the beach, searching for whiting and mackerel. Watching him, Nefyn had learnt to see through the water. To calculate where the stone arch of Porth y Wrach on the headland met the pool where the mackerel idled in August, and to recognize the glassy surface of blue water where the whelks sheltered in winter. To read the bay's hidden language. There were no boats today; the alarms had been sounded and flags raised. Everyone knew the consequences of straying into The Range whilst the military tested their drones. The bay would be closed for weeks at a time and when it was, Nefyn could do nothing but lie sleepless on her bed, listening to the distant thunder of munitions, each strike awakening in her a new depth of dread.

When the military had first come to claim and divide the sea, her father and some of the other fishermen had tried to tell them that the fish moved with the seasons and that leaving them a portion meant nothing. They had claimed to understand, before imposing stricter and stricter conditions, frustrating the fishermen into giving up. Their number dwindled after that, the community scattered. The carcass of her father's boat lay in the boatshed, under a tarpaulin skin. Her brother forced to work on other people's boats on the north coast for weeks at a time before returning home exhausted, only to leave again after just a few days.

Nefyn's eyes flickered upwards to the cliff and the cottage as a light pierced the gloom. Their home clung precariously to the cliff edge above, the sea digging deeper, undercutting the land on which it stood, tipping the house slowly towards it. Her brother would be up now, moving around in the cold, pulling his jumper over his head. Making tea.

Nefyn stopped, her dark eyes scanning the strandline, the daylight growing around her. She bent to pick up an urchin, its paper-thin form luminous in the blue light. She examined it in her fingers for a moment. Its surface was punctured with lines of perforations like the plates of a skull. Her father would say that the tide took the foolish, the reckless and the unlucky. Nefyn had often wondered which one he had been. Her mother had already left them by then, before her father had ventured out to sea on the cusp of a storm. He was found underneath his boat, his body tangled in fishing lines, blue and bloated, his breath whisked away. Perhaps he had been unlucky, she considered, or perhaps the sea had tried to show him all she could and had finally run out of patience.

There was nothing she wanted this morning. She dropped the urchin, listened as it rolled away. She could hear the tide turning, the undercurrents quickening. The sugar kelp which she hung in a ruffled belt on the cottage door had not dried out in days, meaning that this stillness could not last much longer. Something was changing. She could feel it. She turned and walked back up to the cottage, knowing that a storm was near.

2

Gharb • West • Gorllewin

I F HE LAY STILL enough, for long enough on the narrow bed, he could keep himself just below consciousness so that hours would blur into days, and days would fold into weeks, without him being aware of the four walls which held him. He could feel his muscles wasting, his flesh seemed loose about his bones, and the little exercise he was forced to take exhausted him. But if he slowed his breathing in this way, his body would become lighter and he'd feel the touch of his father's palm on the back of his neck and he would be six years old again, learning to swim underneath the Mediterranean sky. Angles of blue and white would fill his mind. He would see his body glistening and strong under the scalding sun. Hear his father whispering, 'Trust me, trust the water, it doesn't want to harm you,' then he would feel his own childlike panic overwhelm him as he grappled for his father's neck, felt himself sinking. On other days, it was the scent of bitter orange that filled his senses, its cloying sweetness drugging him into a welcome stupor, or the buzzing arpeggio of the muezzin's call to prayer.

When consciousness was insistent, he would sit, his back against the cold plaster, his eyes half closed, pushing back the walls with his mind. Like tracing paper, he would overlay memories of his past on to his present. The back wall was the dappled walk beneath the lemon trees towards the university. Past the café where his friends took black tea. The far wall was the corridor where he had first met his wife, the place where she had scolded him sternly for pinning a notice to the wrong board. His flamboyant begging for forgiveness. The bemused look she had given him. The moment he decided he must know more about it and her. The wall behind him was his office, the bricks his books, the muslin drapes that overlooked the city at a time when no one thought to ask what religion their friends were. This bed. This bed was where they had made love without making love. Her white teeth, the way she swore over coffee.

In this way, every day was a day of resurrection. Adding detail, the footfall on the geometric floor of a souk, the laughter of children outside his flat, the stunned flies of summer. And when sleep did overwhelm him, to a dreamless abyss, he'd wake gasping for air and reach for the compass on the bed beside him, the only possession they had allowed him to keep on religious grounds. Hamza had not prayed for years, although he had not told them this. The compass had been a gift from his grandfather when he had come of age. They had smoked shisha together and he had pressed it silently into his palm. They had sat for a while, nothing but the blue smoke and the sound of the bubbling *nargilah*. Hamza had opened the case, looked at the names of the sixteen winds marked on it. Held their names in his mouth for a moment. *Greco. Levante. Scirocco. Osto*. His grandfather had watched him, his aged, damp eyes narrowing as he inhaled the perfumed smoke and suggested to him gently that being a man meant knowing where you were from, knowing where you were going and knowing how to find the *qibla* in order to pray.

He had little sense of time; the windowless cell put paid to any natural rhythms, the only real indication of day and night the changing of the guards outside his cell in eight-hour shifts. A little less noise at night. He knew their footsteps by now. The older guard called Adley, gaunt and irritated, his resentment at being given such a menial job palpable in the agitated flick of his cigarette. When he learnt that Hamza smoked, he pushed a cigarette under the door, knowing full well that Hamza had no way to light it.

But it was the other one that Hamza disliked the most. The younger one they called Owens. He was broader, fair-haired and thickset, his tongue sharp with ambition, a certain swagger appearing in his gait when unwatched by others. Hamza had seen his type at checkpoints. Asking for papers and studying them for too long, disappearing to talk to colleagues in booths, enjoying any discomfort. Thriving on any expression of impatience you made and punishing you for it even though you had committed no crime. He had seen his type a thousand times, making old women wait, frail and tired in the searing sun, simply because they could. But it wasn't Owens walking down the corridor now. Hamza lay listening. It was someone else. An older footfall, heavier, soft-bodied, at once urgent and defeated. He waited for the murmur of voices and the metallic sound of the keys to subside. The door opening. Hamza didn't react. The sound of breathing. A bag being placed on the floor. The weight of the door being locked once again.

'Hamza?'

His voice was hoarse today, his breathing shallow. A silence. Then the sound of footsteps and the cold touch of fingertips on Hamza's inner wrist. The whip of an arm yanking a cuff over a watch face. Silent counting. A calculation. The fingertips disappeared, leaving only the sting of another's touch on his skin. He heard the rasping of the silver chain as the Doctor picked up the compass from the bed, held it in his hands. Dragged the chair towards Hamza and sat.

'I know you can hear me.'

Hamza felt the strangeness of having someone else so near. The Doctor's chest was noisy, as if his haste along the endless, featureless corridors had unsettled it. 'I can't sleep, thinking of you here. Please, Hamza, you have to eat.' Hamza lay unmoving. 'Those sores are getting worse.' The creak of the chair as the Doctor leant closer. The Doctor searched his face for a response. There was none. He lowered his voice conspiratorially. 'Listen to me. They won't force you to eat, Hamza. If you die, you're one less problem for them.'

There was something in this man's voice that made Hamza think of his father. A silence before the sound of his breathing returned once again.

Hamza had been moved. For years. From Syria to Oman, from Oman onwards. Moved and moved so that he had become so far removed from where he had been, who he had been, that he no longer knew himself. Cells. Trucks. Boats. Each country complicating his story. Travelling further and further until he had almost forgotten himself. There had been other medics, too, who were kind enough, but none like this one. This one was older. Perhaps that was it. He was not a military man either. This base seemed smaller, more remote. After so many years, he had, it seemed, reached the end of the line.

Hamza had not spoken to the Doctor for months, the mistrust in which he held his captors at each base constant and unwavering. But one day, the Doctor had told him how his wife had scolded him that morning for snoring. And it had awakened in Hamza a yearning for the ordinary so intense that it had almost broken his heart. After another visit, the Doctor had left him some cake she had made. He'd kept the guard talking long enough that Hamza could eat it. They had begun talking then. Tentatively at first, both skirting the extraordinary circumstances that brought them together, and keeping instead to generalities. Hamza's former post at the university in Homs. His parents' pride at his achievements. The Doctor's life in the nearby village, his visits to the military base made necessary by its size and lack of facilities. And then, in time, when they were surer of each other, they had argued. Hamza challenging the Doctor's hypocrisy, his earnest insistence that he lived in a country with a natural empathy towards the colonized, his discomfort at being both colonized and colonizer. His infuriating rigidity and adherence to what he called his duties, his 'oaths'. The papers he had been forced to sign on beginning his work at the base. His refusal to help Hamza, the ease with which he could have sent word to Hamza's family if he chose to. Their natural liking for each other. Frustrating. Confusing. And in this way, over time, they had forged a fragile, mutual respect. An almost perfect imbalance.

Perhaps, for Hamza, it was knowing he'd decided to end his own life that allowed him to be more open with the Doctor than he had been with all the others. A certain recklessness of feeling that let him speak. And over time, the glimpses the Doctor gave Hamza – of a life lived – made him grieve his own past life so much that it strengthened his resolve, galvanized his decision to retreat.

'Hamza, listen to me. You don't have much time left. I . . . I wouldn't presume to ask for your friendship, but . . .' Hamza felt a hand on his arm. 'We have grown closer and I have tried to pull you back. But there comes a point when your body . . . it won't recover. Your tests, Hamza, they're not good.'

The Doctor allowed the words to settle between them, watched as Hamza's chest rose and fell with a whisper. Their conversations had dwindled over the last weeks, as Hamza continued to refuse food. The Doctor had watched this young man diminish and fall silent as his own inner conflict grew. His cheeks burning with the shame of it. He had tended prisoners before, knew he shouldn't get involved, but as he watched the four walls pushing in on Hamza, he was soon engaged in his own secret war with him, a war to keep him alive. He would find reasons to visit. *Make* reasons to visit, but every time he opened the metal door to his concave features, the deep set of his eyes, a sickness would creep to his stomach. At night, the Doctor would lie wide-eyed, a trembling in his core that spoke of a deep, inward grief. On these evenings, his wife, sensing that he was awake, would lay a gentle hand on his arm and turn to watch her husband stare into the darkness in his helplessness, a tear glistening heavily in the corner of her eye.

He could hear voices in the corridor now. He looked at Hamza's hollow features, his sallow skin. Another sleepless night had preceded this visit, and he had got up at dawn to carry his burden to Hamza. He cleared his throat, his voice suddenly constricted.

'I wanted you to know that my wife . . . my wife and I, we lost a son.' The Doctor felt the words in the air around them, wondering how it was possible for such old words to startle him, to seem so new. 'He was just a boy. He became ill. There was nothing I could do. Perhaps now there would be treatments, but back then . . .' His voice trailed off. He looked down at the compass and felt it warming against his hands. Shook his head, felt his breathing grow shallow.

'Anyway, I could only watch. Wait for the inevitable. But I could come here today, and I *can* ask you, please, *don't* do this. I can't imagine the suffering you have seen, but I can put myself in your parents' place. If you were my son, I'd want you to fight. I'd want you to live. Nothing . . .' he continued, 'nothing has been the same for me or my wife since . . .' The Doctor shook his head, as if to shake off his heaviness. Looked at Hamza's eyes, which remained firmly shut. 'I just wanted to say that, that's all.' He cleared his throat. 'I know more than anyone how easy it is to lose faith.'

A silence fell between them, the Doctor feeling the weight of the compass in his hands. He held it a long time before prising the case open with his fingernail.

It clicked open. Hamza listened to the familiar sound. The Doctor looked at the compass and smiled. The chain lying heavy in his lap. A pause. 'You know they were made to tell your fortune originally . . . wind roses, compasses.' He paused. 'They weren't made to tell direction, they were made to tell you what your future would bring.' He looked at the pin as it spun. Held it flat in the middle of his palm. His brow becoming furrowed. 'Then again, perhaps it's best we don't know. Don't you think?' Hamza heard a soft smile in his voice as he snapped the compass case shut. There were voices outside. Owens. The changing of the guard. The Doctor placed the compass on the bed. Got up. There was a rattling of keys.

'Think about it.' The Doctor pretended to take Hamza's pulse once more. Owens leant into the room and scanned it.

'He's not scheduled a medical visit,' he barked. The Doctor let Hamza's wrist go and gave him a tight smile.

'I know, I was passing. It's part of the medical oath. To keep an eye. You know that, surely.'

Owens studied him. 'Come on,' he said, sparing his elder no civility. The Doctor picked up his bag. Owens stood in the doorway, forcing the Doctor to turn sideways to pass him. The door slammed shut once again, and Hamza's eyes flickered open.

3

Drift ◆ Drifftio ◆ Almaghzaa

'WHERE ARE YOU GOING?' Her brother was stuffing clothes into a waterproof bag. He didn't even look up. 'Joseph?'

'I'll be back in a few weeks.'

Nefyn stood in the bedroom doorway, blocking his path. 'You just came back.'

Joseph shrugged, trying not to look at her.

'I won't be long.'

'But why?' Nefyn searched his face. He turned to find his papers before pushing them into his back pocket. His voice rose sharply.

'We need the money, Nefyn.'

Nefyn's eyes ran everywhere like water. 'It's a girl, isn't it? You didn't used to go so often.'

Joseph stopped for a moment. 'It's not a girl.'

'Just tell me if it is.'

'It's not a girl, I said.' His voice was loud within the confines of the feet-thick stone walls, the low ceilings. 'There's a boat, they're paying well,' he mumbled.

'And you'd rather be anywhere than here.'

'Don't be stupid.'

Nefyn remained in the doorway, a palpable stillness to her. She looked pale this morning, gaunt. Her dark hair almost black. A thin dress. A cardigan. Looking at her, he sometimes couldn't fathom how they had been born together. It had happened at home, their mother determined not to leave the house, and when the midwife eventually arrived and brought him into the world, she placed him quickly aside in order to deliver Nefyn. She had arrived *en caul*, her amniotic sac still intact, completely unaware of the fact that she had been born. Their exhausted mother had looked in on Nefyn's self-contained serenity before the midwife jabbed at the sac that enfolded her. Tore it, much to their mother's anger. It was only then that Nefyn howled, as if she were being killed. Sometimes Joseph wondered whether she had ever really been ready for this world. That night, their father had bought a round of drinks and they rang the bell in the low-beamed bar of The Ship; babies born in water brought great luck.

Joseph noticed that her eyes were still searching his face. His shoulders softened.

'I know it's hard for you, but we've got to buy food.'

When he was younger, he had tried to find work locally, but the questions and the goading soon became intolerable. The fact that he still lived with his sister, the fact that she 'wasn't all there'. He learnt that retaliation brought trouble, and passivity brought more abuse, so it was easier to hitch a ride to the north coast. Work anonymously. Friendly but distant. And it would do for a while, for a week or two, but as the days rolled by, a restlessness would grow in him, a listening-out, more complicated than duty or guilt, until he had to come home. He watched her green eyes become troubled. Fingers picking at fingernails.

'You can't go. There's a storm on the way, I can feel it.'

Joseph rolled his eyes. 'Here we go.'

'It's true, this time.' Her voice faltered. She looked away for a moment. 'I'm sure it is.' Joseph picked up his bag and pushed past her into the narrow kitchen.

'There's plenty of firewood there,' he said. He took some packets of tea, biscuits, pushed them into his bag. Nefyn watched as Joseph took a bottle of pills from his pocket, turning to fill a glass with water. He tipped a tablet out on to his palm and placed it on the wooden table between them. Pushed it towards Nefyn.

'Take it,' he said.

Nefyn studied him with cool eyes, folded her arms, making the most of the little agency she had. She watched a flicker of irritation cross his face. 'Come on,' he coaxed. 'You know they're for your own good.'

Every time he left, he would count out the tablets, place them in a line on the windowsill. One for each day he would be gone. At first, his trips were shorter, less frequent, but now they were becoming routine. She watched him as he tipped the tablets into his palm and laid them out for her one by one. He turned, looked down at the pill, untouched, on the table.

'How many times do we have to do this, Nefyn? They keep you safe,' he urged, his shoulders sinking.

'They keep *me* safe?' Nefyn could sense his growing impatience, his desire to leave.

'I wouldn't give them to you if I didn't think they helped.'

Nefyn smiled coldly. Studied him. Joseph could feel his anger at the back of his throat. The walls of the cottage starting to weigh on him.

'They don't help, they make me feel nothing, Joseph.'

'But that's better. Don't you think?' Nefyn looked suddenly unsure. He recognized the loose thread in her demeanour, started to unpick her resolve. 'It is, isn't it?' he assured. 'You know it is.' She was unravelling and he could feel it. 'And anyway, the days will go quicker this way. Until I'm back.'

He'd won again; he could sense it. He watched as Nefyn tentatively reached out her hand and picked up the tablet, placed it on her tongue. Joseph pushed the glass of water towards her, his gaze dropping. 'We're running low, I'll get some more when I'm gone,' Joseph said, as he pushed the bottle back into his pocket. He watched her drink. 'I've asked Efa to bring you food. Let her put the box on the bench outside. Don't let her in, OK?'

Nefyn nodded. 'All right.'

Joseph stood for a moment. The girl he was seeing would be waiting for him. He'd met her at the harbourside in the North. She was working in one of the cafés there. She didn't know about Nefyn, of course. He wouldn't, after all, ever bring her back here, but she allowed him to be someone else, for a while at least. Nefyn was still, the relaxant beginning to work. He found himself pressing her to him for a moment, and kissing her head, before hauling his bag over his shoulder and leaving without looking back.

After he had gone, Nefyn pulled a blanket around her and went to sit on the bench that overlooked the cove. Whoever had built the whitewashed cottage knew to build it shoulder to the wind, keeping the windows on the less exposed side of the house. This meant that although you could feel the sea's reverberations in the cottage, its sound and thin light, you could not see it. There were only four rooms: two bedrooms, low-ceilinged and cramped, a tiny kitchen and a living room with a fireplace and a slate floor. Perhaps, at one time, there had been a garden in front of the cottage, but it had been lost to the sea, inch by inch, tide by tide, so that now there was only room for a bench jostling for space amongst the lobster pots and piled-up floats. The sea had flooded the cove by now, deadening the sound of the shale, the water too full and heavy to make much noise.

Nefyn sat feeling her muscles soften, and watched as the water changed colour. Her mother had always teased them when they were children by asking them what colour the water was. How it seemed grey in winter, and black before a squall, how it was colourless over their feet in the shallows and stained indigo after a storm. She would laugh at them and say it could be any colour and no colour at all. Nefyn almost felt her cheek on hers as she whispered that the best questions had no answers. Although the morning light had strengthened, Nefyn had no expectations for what today would bring. The next few weeks would be measured out in a line of round white tablets. She closed her eyes and waited for the days to slip by.

4

Hikma ✦ *Wisdom* ✦ *Doethineb*

HAMZA HAD STARTED EATING. He had spent the first night – after the little bread that he had pushed into his mouth – lying on the floor of his cell, his body and bowel fighting against the food. In the early hours, he had pulled himself up and sat back against the bed, his throat burning with retching, his face damp with sweat as he waited for more spasms in his gut. He hallucinated, too, and saw a man who looked like his father but with the Doctor's hands. And he had cried. Something he hadn't done since he was first incarcerated in the first prison in the first country, not because of fear for his own safety, or pride, but because the outpouring of grief was so great, it was too much, and had become stuck in his throat. Each agony suspended. But now he had started weeping as he sat on the floor of his cell, forcing himself to live. He had pushed his face into the sheets and howled, realizing that freeing himself through death had now become an impossibility too.

A few days had passed since then, and as he mechanically ate the food offered to him, sometimes he'd vomit, or soil the bed without warning, as if his body had already made up its mind to die. Owens would curse him, then make him strip the sheets, but would leave them in the cell for long enough that the acrid smell would catch the back of Hamza's throat, making him retch once more.

His mind had a new clarity; he would be awake for longer periods, his conscious thoughts becoming more ordered, his feelings sharpening. He knew that this was the only way, but it took him further and further from the memories that sustained him. Disappearing became harder, the food that fuelled his body turning his mind outwards. And when he yearned to lie down, to close his eyes once again, he would force his fingertips to reach for his inner wrist, searching again for signs of life, his tender pulse.

His body seemed to grow around him, the more he wore it. The more he came back to himself. The ribs that Fatima had played like a piano, when they had first married. Her fingers finding notes in his bones, his flesh. The stomach that she used to lay her head on to listen to the universe inside him. His jaw, the same jaw that she struck that one time when he unintentionally insulted her brother. The jaw with which he had failed to apologize and the hands that he had used to repair a cupboard for her. An indirect atonement. Oblique. This, after all, had always been his way with women. His father had told him never to look directly at the sun, and Fatima, he would soon learn, was equally full of fire and heat.

When he'd stated his intention to get married, he had been taken to see his uncle who possessed *hikma*. His uncle spoke of the family's surprise at the suddenness of his decision. Told him a tale of a man who had married in haste and repented at leisure. Hamza had laughed, thanked him and married Fatima anyway. They had stayed in bed for a week after their wedding. Her appetite shocked and delighted him. The swearing. She enjoyed lying on the cushioned floor, the windows flung open. Smoking. He had not asked her if he was her first, not because he did not want to know the answer, but because he already knew it. They had slept together as the rain fell on the red earth outside, her limbs musky with the scent of laurel soap. For a moment, he swore that he could feel the weight of her head on his collarbone.

There were older reminders, too, on his flesh. The scars on his knees from when he fell flying kites with his brother when they were children. The fierce competition between them. His brother's athletic ability, his own scholarly ambitions. The soft shoulders his father had leant his arm upon the day Hamza completed his education. The way his father did not speak of his pride after the dinner their mother had prepared that evening, but showed it in his gentle teasing of his sons, the way he touched his wife's hand as she cleared the dishes. Then there was the knee, the knee his bachelor friend had ceremonially pricked with a needle the morning of his wedding to Fatima, in the hope that he too would soon find himself a bride. Hamza felt the history of his flesh around him once more. His limbs numb and heavy as if life, in its return, wanted to sting him with its strength, show him how far he would have to come. He sat in his dirty clothes, his thoughts centring on Fatima.

He had tried to be what she wanted, to say what she wanted him to, but she became like a book in a language unknown to him. He could see the marks on the page, where sentences and paragraphs fell, but he did not understand her. She blamed it on his upbringing, the coldness of his mother, but Hamza had never thought his mother cold. She just did not waste her words. Fatima disappeared between his arms. He stopped sleeping. Became critical. She would be loyal, of course, but one day he caught her washing their clothes, a stillness about her as she hung them on the line to dry, as if setting out her family or an approximation of who they were under the sun, and his heart ached for her although he would never say as much. So, they had held their son between them, held him up to the light and watched as he bound them together in their admiration. They would tell him stories. Weave their words around him so that all three would be spellbound, as present in the story as they were absent from the real world. Hamza felt again for his pulse under his fingertips. The breakfast he had eaten making him nauseous, his whole body aching with the decision to live.

The door opened.

'Come on.' It was Owens. His uniform pressed. Hamza thought he was there to collect the breakfast tray, but no. 'I said, come on!' Hamza stood up, his legs adjusting a moment, kept his head low as the blood rushed to it. He moved towards the door, brushed past him. 'You stink,' Owens muttered.

The corridor was anonymous, with each one leading to yet another unremarkable pathway. As a mapmaker, he knew a little about the design. How they exploited the natural landscape. How sites were chosen that were favourable. Privacy was always at a premium. This seemed to be common to all countries. Accessible but not vulnerable. Sprawling, rather than clustered, to minimize damage if attacked. Access to a low-skilled local workforce who would not ask too many questions. Hamza stopped at the closed door, waited for Owens to slide a key card over a scanner. The door opened.

'Left!' the soldier barked. He had not been this way before. He was usually shown to a cage, covered, no bigger than a tennis court. He waited again. Another card. Another door. Losing his bearings. He had edged off the map in his mind. And then, a small bare-earth exercise yard. A fence around the perimeter. Owens nodded him through. Adley was there already, leaning on the wire mesh, standing guard, smoking.

'There's been a change, new directives.' Hamza stood, not listening, the cold air knifing through his regulation shirt. The noise was deafening. The sound of the waves below the cliff all-consuming after the silence of his cell. He could taste the salt in the air. For the first time in years he could see the sky. Not gridded by mesh, sectioned. The whole expanse, vast and voluminous.

'They're allowing you time to pray, four times a day now.' Owens was watching him. Hamza was still looking upwards. 'Did you hear me?!'

Hamza tried to centre his attention on him. Out here he looked smaller, nothing more than a boy. He saw him moving closer to him, could feel his warm breath on his face.

'I said, did you hear me?'

Hamza hadn't used his voice in weeks.

'I . . . I . . . don't pray.' It didn't sound like his voice any more. Owens let out a bitter laugh.

'Four times a day for you lot, that's what they said.'

'You lot?' Hamza whispered under his breath.

'Yes. You lot.'

Hamza watched him.

'But I don't pray, and if I did, I could pray inside . . .' Hamza noticed Owen's jaw clenching. The breeze catching his fair hair.

'I don't make the fucking rules. I just follow them. And if I say you'll pray then you'll fucking pray.' Hamza's eyes were adjusting to the light. He noticed that Owens had freckles across the bridge of his nose and his temples, his skin young, like one of Hamza's students.

'What are you looking at?' His eyes were steely grey. Flint-like. Easy to ignite. Perhaps it was the light but there seemed to be a sepia tone to everything. A redness in the sky.

'It's just . . . the cold.'

Owens studied him, conscious of Adley's gaze.

'Go on, then.' He was waiting. Hamza was light-headed, his breathing shallow. The cries of gulls overhead strange and threatening. 'I said, GO ON!' The boy was shouting now. Hamza pulled at the chain around his neck, lifted it over his head. Tried to centre himself, find Mecca. His fingertips were freezing. The wind seemed brutal. He couldn't get the pin to settle. It seemed to move as he laid the compass flat on his palm. He sensed Owens's fury growing but the pin would not find direction. He turned around to see if it would help. The wind was strengthening. Hamza could feel it pulling on him, on his clothes. It was no good.

Then, he felt the baton on the back of his knees and his legs buckled. The compass dropped to the floor. Hamza gasped. The touch of the earth raw and startling. Owens bent over and picked up the compass. Hamza's head snapped up.

'Give it back to me.' His voice came from somewhere deep inside.

Owens half smiled.

'I said, give it back.'

'If you want it back, pray.' He spat out the words slowly, deliberately.

A sudden heat flashed through Hamza's body. The boy closed in on him.

'Come on, then.'

Hamza clenched his jaw. Swallowed down his rage.

'I said, come on, then!'

Hamza looked up at him, his hands trembling. Tried to push him away with his mind. The heat still coursing through his body. He tried to steady his breath, raised his hands to his ears.

'*Allahu Akbar*.' He looked down, his lips trying to find the words. He drew them up from deep inside like water from a well, more from instinct, the need to survive, than from memory. Then they dried up. Evaporated in his mouth. Owens was circling him now.

'*Allahu Akbar* . . .' He tried to centre his attention on his intent to pray. '*Subhana Rabbiyal A'la* . . .'

Owens's boots on the gravelly soil.

'I can't hear you!'

'*Subhana Rabbiyal A'la . . .*'

'I said, I can't hear you!'

Adley threw down his cigarette, interested now.

Every time Owens passed Hamza's face, he would swing the compass carelessly. Dangerously. Hamza tried to bring his mind back to the prayer. Fragments of words he had repeated a thousand times. Words that once were like bread. Sustenance. Taught to him by his grandfather. Gently. Words that he had formed as he was taught to speak so that prayers and language were intertwined. But now they lay broken on his tongue. Retreating further with Owens's every irritated step. Owens was sneering at him. Hamza bowed in *sujood*, touched the ground with his forehead for a moment before raising himself to sitting again. He looked up at the guard.

The boy looked down at him.

'Was that it?'

Hamza remained silent. Owens pressed open the case, looked at the inscriptions before glancing over at Adley and smiling. 'This doesn't even make any sense.'

Hamza waited. Somehow, he knew it would happen, even before it did. It was a sharp movement. Instinctive. Like the sticking of a knife. The chain and the weight of the compass gave him leverage and Hamza watched as he threw it, over the railings and into the sea.

Hamza didn't feel anything at all. Perhaps he was still too weak. Perhaps it was because he had seen so much of humanity's cruelty that his disgust was deadened. He calmly got to his feet and approached the boy. Considered the frightening liveliness in his eyes, the triumph. He was breathing hard. Hamza tilted his head.

'I feel sorry for you,' he said quietly, 'so sorry.' The boy's smile straightened slowly.

Hamza was walking away when the first blow hit him on the back of his skull. There was the sudden metallic taste of blood in his mouth. He fought back, but his body was heavy and the boy had struck first. He tried to hold him off by his neck, and did not hear the kick which shattered his ribs, for by then he was unconscious.

5

Squall • 'asfa • Tymestl

T HE SEA WAS TROUBLED. Efa stood in the empty house and looked out across the harbour. The wind had mewled like an infant this morning as she walked along the sea wall. She could hear it now, rattling the windowpanes irritably. She checked that the old sash window was properly locked and closed the curtains.

She had ten houses in her care, each of which she visited once a week for their owners. Other than for a few weeks a year, the houses that looked over the harbour would remain empty, until summer brought them to mind again. In the meantime, Efa was paid to tend them, like graves. They were beautiful houses, too beautiful for any local wages to buy. When Efa was a child, she knew the names of everyone who lived here, played with their children. Would be in and out of people's houses. Now they looked unfamiliar, dressed in coastal colours, even their old names erased or changed by owners who did not wish to learn them. She pulled her coat around her. Although well maintained, the houses were unheated at this time of year.

It was as if the village were sick. In summer, the owners came from cities, formed a village of their own. Cafés and hotels would swell with their numbers. Local men drinking from tankards at the end of bars would disappear amongst families and noise and dogs. The village would then feign life, its cheeks falsely rouged by laughter and abandon before September took them away, leaving café staff staring from windows and ice-cream kiosks closed. The village would turn inwards then, almost embarrassed by the gaiety it had fallen for.

When the plans for the military base were unveiled, there had been promises of year-round investment, but although a few of the younger men worked there as cleaners and guards, the base was self-sufficient. Hermetically sealed. Efa walked across the tasteful wooden floor and stepped into the hall. She listened to the house a moment. It was silent. She turned and opened the door, making sure to lock it behind her.

It was the birds that she noticed first. They were flying inland. Dozens of them, and although the sea was fairly calm, the winds seemed to be criss-crossing its surface in an agitated way. She looked upwards before checking her watch. She would need to get back to Emrys soon. She only had one chore left for this morning.

∽

The two guards sat outside the Lieutenant Colonel's office. There were murmurings inside as he and the Captain discussed the case. When the door opened, they snapped to their feet and saluted. The Captain nodded them through.

The office was more like a civilian one than many others on the base. Owens had only been summoned there previously to be informed of successes and promotions. There was a picture of the Lieutenant Colonel's wife and family on the desk. Books. He looked up at Owens, his fingers intertwined on the desk. He observed the guards for a moment.

'So?' he said. 'Which one of you two is going to tell me what happened?'

He waited. Studied their respective faces.

'The exercise yard is overseen by cameras, but it seems that the CCTV . . .' he chose his words carefully, 'was misaligned.'

The Lieutenant Colonel was sure he saw a suggestion of a smirk on Owens's face. He regarded him. Let a moment pass.

'Anyone?' he asked. He looked at some notes on his desk, leant back on his chair, looked away. 'You see, gentlemen, I'm particularly irritated because this prisoner was sent here into our care by General Reeves and he's going to want to know what happened to him.'

The Captain had retreated to the far end of the room, looking out of the window, keeping a respectful distance.

'Adley?'

The older man tried not to flinch at the sudden mention of his name. The words he and Owens had exchanged as they dragged Hamza back to his cell. Hamza had had it coming.

'What have you got to say for yourself?'

'Nothing, sir.'

The Lieutenant Colonel considered this.

'He's badly injured. Three broken ribs. And since we haven't got the facilities for him here, we're duty-bound to move him to a larger base with a hospital wing.' He looked back at Owens. Measured him with his eyes. 'You have a clean record. Exemplary.'

'Thank you, sir.' Owens shifted his weight slightly. Cleared his throat.

'He was weak. Clearly no match for either of you.' Owens said nothing. 'I don't like unnecessary force.' Owens let his eyes fall on the crown that adorned the Lieutenant Colonel's shoulder. 'It's degrading for everyone involved.'

The Lieutenant Colonel studied their stubborn silence. Drew an intake of breath.

'OK, so here's what's going to happen: you have forty-eight hours to tell me who beat him, otherwise we'll put you both in the guardroom pending court martial.'

Adley's eyes darted to Owens, who laughed bitterly.

'I'm sorry?' the Lieutenant Colonel asked sharply.

'He's nothing but scum. Scum that killed our soldiers,' said Owens under his breath.

'You know nothing of his involvement in any conflict and I urge you to remember who you're speaking with.' The Lieutenant Colonel's voice wavered dangerously.

'We're not even supposed to be holding him,' spat Owens.

The Lieutenant Colonel felt the weight of his words. Knew their implication. He sat back. A near-admiration for this young man's cockiness. 'I don't know what you're talking about.'

'With respect, sir, I think you do.'

The Lieutenant Colonel smiled tightly.

'It's *your* conduct in this matter that will be under scrutiny.'

'But a court martial for either of us would blow it wide open. The whole business.'

Owens could tell he was getting to him. The Lieutenant Colonel straining to keep his voice even. Authoritative.

'You have forty-eight hours. Have a think about your careers and what you'd like to sacrifice for your little "friendship".'

The Captain had come to stand near them now, was studying their faces. Owens smiled. Didn't look away.

'Yes, sir,' they said.

∽

Joseph had asked Efa to leave the box of food on the bench, but every time Efa called she knocked. Years ago, she had hoped each time that someone would answer. Would prepare herself by smoothing down her hair, patting her skirt. But as the years went by, no one ever did.

Efa had known Nefyn's father, had grown up in the village with him. Shared the intimacy that only knowing someone as a child could bring. She had never liked him, but there was only one schoolroom, everyone together, and in such a small village there was no escape. She had been surprised when he married; he was the sort that fathers warned their daughters about. Heavy-handed. Rough. And it was such an unlikely match.

Efa and her husband had themselves tried for children and their failure had turned to sadness, and sadness to silence. When Joseph and Nefyn's father drowned, and with their mother already gone, she sought to do then what made sense to her: to think about their well-being. Joseph had his father's strength, the kind of resilience that came when you lived somewhere where the trees stayed small and leant away from the wind. It was Nefyn she worried about. She was a strange thing, beautiful in her own way but reserved. She wouldn't speak when she was small, spent all her time in the cove. As she grew, she withdrew more and more so that nobody ever really saw her.

Efa had taken it upon herself to bring Nefyn clothes, ask about her education. She always tried to corner Joseph but, afraid of overstepping the mark, she had learnt to do only what was asked of her. Neighbours had questioned her in the past about her involvement, fearful that she was being taken advantage of, as she seemed to get so very little in return. But Efa gained someone else to think of, and for her, that was enough. Over the years, she had become more and more defensive and given terse replies so that now, people very rarely asked.

Efa remembered seeing Nefyn once, on one of her own long walks along the coast, when it was safe to leave Emrys alone. The girl was waist-deep in water, looking into the distance, completely still. The current swirling around her. Birds tumbling overhead. Efa stopped, her heart leaping, out of breath. Nefyn hadn't noticed that anyone was there and she stood, her back against the cove, as if she were listening. Listening to something that Efa could not hear. She wondered whether she should shout but she didn't. She just watched her, her dark hair moving on her shoulders, her slight figure feeling the force of the sea, before slowly turning for home.

Efa waited by the door. Felt the wind pulling at her. She had placed a warm cardigan in with the food she had bought. Something she had knitted from an emerald-green wool flecked with wisps of blue. Joseph would give her money for food, of course, but she would not take any for anything else. He would call the house from his lodging in the North, leave part of his wages in brown envelopes outside the cottage. It was difficult for him too, Efa knew that. He was young. They were both young. The wind whipped around her ears, and Efa felt the grip of the cold in her arthritic bones. She sighed, happier now that Nefyn would be fed at least, before turning back towards her car.

6

Storm ◆ Storom ◆ Easifuh

D AWN HAD ALREADY SET out its colours over the sea. The light was thick. Nefyn had been awake all night, having slept too much the day before. She hadn't eaten either but came down to the cove to watch the morning colours unfold. The sky was red. Not crimson or scarlet, but a dark blood red. The indigo clouds gathering. She had known, deep down, that she was right.

Its birth would have been hundreds and thousands of miles away. A ripple. A disturbance on the sea that didn't settle. Something that couldn't be let go, and the warmth of the sun would magnify it into wind. And the wind would worry it until the waves and the swell would make the whole world feel as if it were moving. And its approach would be imperceptible at first. The tone of the breeze would change. A sound under a sound. A strange insistence. The rattle of the glass cabinets in the cottage. The disappearance of the birds. The deadening of the sea as the weight of the storm rolled in, a deep, disconcerting inhalation of the sky . . .

Nefyn hadn't taken her tablet this morning, and seemed somehow unable to catch her breath. She had lain, her pupils wide, feeling the prickling all over her skin. Then, she had risen, started pacing, unable to eat or drink, stopping every now and again to hold her breath and listen. She could hear it. She was sure she could hear it. It was in the echo of the sky.

When she arrived down at the cove, the strandline was subdued, quiet. The headlands reaching. The tide receding. The rocks dark and damp. She had stood, a tremor inside her, her cold skin mottled in the morning chill. Every sense alive. The only movement was a lone cormorant left behind, drying its wings on the rocks near by. She smiled, knew there wouldn't be much longer to wait.

The Doctor inverted the vial, drew down the painkiller and pinched the skin on Hamza's bicep before injecting it. Hamza looked at him, his eyes heavy.

'It'll help with the pain when you're moved.'

Hamza nodded. The Doctor rubbed his skin to take away the sting. The army truck had been parked outside the nearest doorway, but it was still a long walk and there was no wheelchair.

'I don't know why they didn't get a proper ambulance.' The Doctor's voice reverberated with anger. Hamza smiled.

'Don't you?'

The Doctor packed his bottles away. Snapped his case shut in irritation. Hamza watched him.

'I can't believe they did this to you.' His voice was tight in his throat. Hamza studied him. 'It's barbaric.' Hamza watched him seethe. Let him settle.

'I suppose we are going to part ways,' Hamza said, the opiate starting to spread in his system. 'I've . . .'

Hamza searched for the word, '*appreciated* our talks.'
The Doctor smiled, looked away.

'I'm sorry I couldn't have done more.'

Hamza considered this. Shrugged. 'You did everything you thought you could.'

The Doctor took this in. Watched as Hamza's figure succumbed to the drug in his system. His eyes and shoulders softening.

Hamza reached out his hand, placed it gently on the Doctor's forearm.

'I am so sorry for what happened to your son,' Hamza said. The Doctor felt the sting of tears in his throat.

'You were listening?'

'Of course.'

'You know we have this tradition here, us old people; it's called *hebrwng*. When friends come to visit us, when we're their hosts, we walk back with them half the way.' The Doctor smiled sadly. 'It's our way of making sure they're well on their way home safely.'

'Please, don't trouble yourself.'

The old man shook his head.

'Please, let me come with you. I just want to make sure your conditions are suitable. That's all. Let me do that for you.' His voice was breaking.

Hamza nodded imperceptibly.

The door swung open, making them both start. It was Adley.

'Is he ready?' His voice was edged with impatience.

The Doctor shrugged, looked to Hamza.

'Are you?'

Hamza breathed in deeply before hauling himself to his feet. He gasped in involuntary agony and stumbled as the elderly doctor shouldered his weight. Held him up. His arm about the younger man's waist, their faces close together.

'Come on, my friend,' he said gently. 'I'll help you.'

Nefyn lay on her bed, listening to the storm engulf the house. The weight of the wind, the way it shuddered inland from afar. Below the cottage the waves had begun to hit the bottom of the cove walls. Vibrating. Thundering. Each wave accompanied by an echo, an insistent, disconcerting bass note. Not violent yet, but knocking. Testing. The petulant wind had started to whistle too, sounding out the angles of the cottage. When the rain began it was a sodden mist swirling, dampening, wetting the lungs when inhaled. Lacing eyelashes and foreheads. Now, the mist had thickened, was more tangible somehow. Sharp droplets thrown by gusts. Nefyn listened as it rattled against the roof tiles. Watched as the old curtains swayed in the draught from the aged window frames.

Nothing stayed the same, she knew that. Dunes moved. Boats sank. Cottages succumbed to the sea. Coves changed shape, but there was a certain thrill to the clinging. The listening in the dark. Not knowing in what form change would come. Waiting on the precipice as the sea undercut everything you held dear. The glass cabinets were rattling more now, the fragile forms they contained vibrating with a frequency she could almost hear. Deep down in the cove, the force of the waves was getting stronger, as if growing bolder against the coast's weakness. Sensing its lack of resistance. She could hear shingle being lifted and turned by the waves, worked in a mechanical process, ruthlessly efficient.

Her mother had loved storms as much as her father had hated them. He could see nothing but lost money, damage and fear. When they shouted at each other, he was often at a loss. Uncomprehending eyes. Slamming doors. Nefyn used to go to her mother and rest her head on her knee and eventually her mother would stroke it. In their stillness she could find a way to her. But when her father beat her mother, her flesh darkening under his fists, making her wince as she lowered herself to bathe, it wasn't so easy. She would hide herself so that Nefyn wouldn't see, wouldn't allow her to sleep under her nightdress as she had done as an infant. The bruising visible in the way she walked, in the way she smiled. Pleasing but not pleased. That's why Nefyn thought she enjoyed the storms. Because her father hated them and because they probably reminded him that some things were stronger than he was.

It had taken an hour to walk the corridor to the exit, the Doctor steadfastly ignoring Adley's irritation. Encouraging Hamza to rest periodically in order to let the painkiller take a better hold. The wind whipped the door from Adley's hands when they eventually reached the outside, making him swear profusely. His eagerness to see the back of Hamza palpable. The

Doctor instinctively took off his coat and, holding it above Hamza, shielded him as best he could.

By the time Hamza and the Doctor were seated in the back of the truck, it was dark. Rain had begun to move in sheets, sideways across the base. Their backs and shoulders were soaked through. Hamza closed his eyes against the pain and leant the back of his head against the side of the truck. The Doctor rolled up his wet jacket, pushed it against Hamza's ribs for protection. Hamza opened his eyes. The Doctor coming in and out of focus as he rummaged for a handkerchief from his pocket to dry his face. He was breathing heavily. Both of them were. Then, when the Doctor was sure that Hamza was as comfortable as he could be, he banged on the side of the truck with his fist until they heard the engine ignite. The Doctor watched Hamza's face as they drove over speed bumps at the checkpoints to the base. It was dark again in the back of the truck save for the square of orangey light that penetrated from the window between the back and the cab. Dark figures in the front. Adley, his feet already up on the dashboard, the driver next to him. Paperwork. Permissions. Radioed instructions and the metallic scrape of the electric gate opening. The wind was putting pressure on the side of the truck, the driver sometimes over-correcting. And then, the surge of the engine as they found the coast road.

The winds screamed around the cottage. Nefyn watched as her specimens shifted in the cabinets. Clustering.

Diverging. Some shelves had come loose, glass squares shattering as they fell on to the shelf below, scattering objects everywhere. Her mind, her head, was full to bursting and for the first time in years, she felt dangerously alive.

She walked towards the wooden door and let it open without bracing against it. She gasped as the storm came to meet her, embraced her. She moved along the side of the cottage wall as the gale seemed to replace her breath with its own. Breathing her in. She stood for a moment, preparing herself. Her back against the cottage. She could feel its walls trembling. Could feel the ground beneath her shifting. Then, she turned the corner and stepped to face the full force of the wind and the rain. She allowed the wind to hold her on the precipice of the cliff. The dark waves down below thundering around the cove. She closed her eyes. Her hair whipping, the wind pulling at her dress. The waves were higher than she'd ever seen them, dark and surging, rolling violently.

Nefyn stood still as, five miles along the coast, the cliffside gave way. The road crumbled, tipping a truck sideways, throwing Hamza and the Doctor into each other's arms. The sound of a landslide. Glass breaking. The world falling. The plunge into water. The whites of eyes, terrified. Then, the profound silence as the icy cold engulfed them.

7

Shell ◆ Cragen ◆ Alsudaf

Efa HAD SPENT THE night comforting Emrys. He had insisted that they keep the lamp on and had lain awake all night, his arms tightly wrapped around her waist like a child, his mind far away. Efa had left him in bed this morning and had walked downstairs to the particular silence that only the aftermath of a storm brought. The light was luminous and transparent. Thin. She looked out at the harbour, where figures milled around. The first ones out assessing the damage. She had watched Emrys's face all night, tried to quell the abject fear there. Anchor him to her. She had felt his body relax this morning, his arms loosening around her, and she knew from his breathing that he was asleep. Pushed his arms away and rolled him on to his side.

He had stopped trying to make love to her now. Stopped touching her in her sleep. The confusion and forgetting had been easier somehow; it was the reaching out for her in the dark that broke her heart. They had been young once, of course. She even remembered being caught by his older brother making love in the back of Emrys's car. But all that had faded after the ache of the miscarriages, after the endless conversations in which they tried to prove to each other – to themselves – that with each new pregnancy, nothing could be certain. And then the practised, philosophical acceptance of each lost child, when all that they felt was cold, empty grief.

Perhaps the freedom of not being able to have children could have allowed them some pleasure in lovemaking; instead, its tantalizing possibility destroyed their hunger. It was a shock, then, for Efa, when he started reaching out again. And she had reciprocated once or twice, needing to be close to him in body if not in mind, and out of guilt. She was glad that all that had passed, and she had found a strange tenderness in being able to hold him now like a child. She turned. His voice. He was calling her. Scared that she had gone. She filled the kettle. Thought about the houses in her care and wondered whether she should call on Nefyn. She had never known a storm like that. So all-consuming. So merciless.

The birds were back. Their shrieks loud against the spent sea. The violence of its outburst was evident in the uprooted trees that littered the bay. Rocks, impossible to lift, had been tossed around like pebbles. Driftwood scattered everywhere. The birds were making the most of food brought up from the depths. The sea was stained dark, as it always was after a storm. Endless agitation having changed its very nature and composition. The waves rippled guiltily this morning, their energy lost, the breeze gentle and even. Apologetic. Contrite. Like a man the morning after beating his wife.

∽

Nefyn's eyes opened, found focus. Her hair was wet, her skin salty. Her bones ached. She had made her way back inside and was lying amongst the broken glass of the cabinets. The door was still open, banging occasionally in the morning breeze. She tried to move. She had cuts on her arms. She pulled herself to sit, shivering. The windows were still intact, but there were pools of water on the floor from the leaking roof. Despite the destruction, she felt a strange calm.

She pulled herself up to standing and unpicked a shard of glass from the skin of her forearm. Let it drop to the floor. She tested her walk, moved towards the kitchen, leant her back on the doorframe and looked over at the row of tablets waiting for her. Then she thought of the one who put them there, furrowed her brow, drew him near to her in her mind. He was safe. She could feel it. Ever since they had been in the womb together, she always knew deep down whether he was in trouble. She had only felt her heart lurch once, when he had gone with some friends to leap off the rocks at Porth y Wrach and started showing off. She had run there from the cottage, shouting. Knowing there was something wrong. Arrived to find him standing on the arch, waiting to jump. He had been furious, his friends falling about with laughter. He had hauled her away by her arm, swearing. She had seen him, though, in her mind, blood running down his face, his chest; his friends, the ones that were laughing now, pale-faced and panicked. She considered the tablets a moment, before turning and walking barefoot over the broken glass towards the door.

The cove was at once strange and familiar. Changed but the same. Boulders had moved, seaweeds ripped from rockfaces. The boatshed door had split on one side. Nefyn let her feet find the shale, allowed it to ground her. It was a slack-water sea far away. Lines of debris washed further up the beach than usual. She would find extraordinary things after storms. Blind fish, their forms grotesque and bulging, from distant worlds. Bottles. Seeds from shores at the other side of the globe. Her eyes scanned the strandline. There would be seaweeds that only grew in deep water, and kelp. Molluscs, their tongues lolling, egg cases and shells. Jumbled together in a mass of living things. Summer storms would bring drifts of jellyfish, gelatinous and stranded, and Nefyn's favourites, the by-the-wind sailors, blue when found, then fragile and papery when kept. They spent their whole lives being carried by currents and blown by the wind. There would be sea spume, too, creamy and voluminous, rolling in clouds along the tideline.

Nefyn bent, the blood drying on her arms, and picked at some seaweed to find its texture soft. She drew her hand back, her eyes finding a form in the debris. She looked again. Pulled the seaweed away. Her mind slow to complete the picture. It was a man. Dark hair straggly. A swollen face. Bruising. She stared, tracing the shape of his back, his legs, his arms in the flotsam. She gasped. Her breathing shallow. She reached out her hand, touched the skin of his face. He was still warm. She stepped back, heart heaving in her chest, and looked around and up, scanned the line of the cliff, but there was no one else. She dropped to her knees, raked the debris from his body with her fingers, his shape becoming clearer. She got to her feet, held his upper arm in one hand, his forearm in the other, and anchored her weight against him. He was heavy. She readjusted her hold, pulled once more and, slowly, he started to move. She straightened her back and started pulling, pulling him up the beach towards the boathouse.

8

Boat • Cwch • Qarib

THE LIEUTENANT COLONEL PRESSED his thumb against the lighter. Tilted his head. Nothing but a spark. He tried again. Again. A flame at last. He tipped his head back, inhaled, threw the lighter down on to the desk. The Captain stood in front of the desk, watching him, bracing himself. He declined the offer of a cigarette.

'We recovered the driver and the guard. The medic's body is being taken to the morgue as we speak,' the Captain said, his voice as tense as his manner.

The Lieutenant Colonel rubbed his forehead with his thumb.

'Jesus Christ,' he muttered. He flicked some ash into an ashtray on the desk. Narrowed his eyes. 'And what exactly are we going to tell the Doctor's wife?' he asked.

The Captain looked down. Shrugged.

'I understand that this is going to be difficult.'

The Lieutenant Colonel leant both hands on the back of his chair, lowered his voice conspiratorially.

'Questions have been asked. You know as well as I do that Whitehall have been pressuring us about transparency.'

'He's dead.'

'Is he?'

'He must be.' The Captain shrugged. 'I'd say it was problem solved.'

The older man considered this.

'In his condition? He could never have survived it,' the Captain mused.

'Even so, what if his body turns up somewhere? Along the coast?'

The Captain shrugged again.

'He's a refugee. A stowaway. From a boat. No one will care. We can have a word with the police. Make sure they're on board.'

The Lieutenant Colonel's eyes were drawn to the picture of his wife, his children. He moved around the chair, sat down heavily.

'This has been a bloody nightmare from beginning to end.' He stubbed out the cigarette roughly. Rubbed his face with the palms of his hands. 'It had to happen to this one; you know how the General feels about him. Bloody hell . . .' He sighed deeply. 'Send some people out to make discreet enquiries . . . civilian clothes, of course . . .'

The Captain nodded.

'We'll keep them away from the site anyway for a few weeks,' he continued. 'The road has collapsed. The coast road is closed. That's easily explained.

'We'll have to put out a statement locally; we'll field questions from GCHQ afterwards. We're so close to delivery of the drones. Any questions about our competency at this point in time wouldn't be helpful. You know how much investment there's been in this.'

The Captain nodded again, knew that he knew as much as they wanted him to.

'He's dead. That's all that matters.'

The Lieutenant Colonel could barely disguise his irritation.

'Well, let's bloody hope so.'

Nefyn had laid him inside her father's broken boat. Tried to warm him with the sail. Then she had run all the way up the path to the cottage to fetch some of Joseph's warm clothes and some water. She dragged the broken door closed behind her. He was still unconscious. She stepped into the boat beside him and placed a hand on his breastbone. He was cold now. Very cold. She set to work unbuttoning his shirt. Its thin blue material looked like a uniform, a row of numbers on a breast pocket. She pulled him towards her and pushed the sodden fabric over his shoulder before her eyes slid to the bruising on his side. He was thin. Dark maroon sores on the bottom of his spine. The bruising started under his arm and extended the length of his torso. She rolled him over again and removed his shirt, trying not to let him fall back on to the wooden boat. Joseph's shirts were thick, heavy. She gathered the fabric, a sleeve in her hand, and pulled his fingers through before pushing the shirt on to his arm. She slid the material behind him before doing the same with his other arm. Her fingers were trembling with cold as she fumbled with the buttons. Painstakingly, she changed his clothes, her heart sinking at every bruise. She rolled his thin hips from side to side, covering him. Looking away as she worked, knowing he was getting colder and colder. Then, when she had finished, she folded a

48

blanket under his head and around his body and sat back on her knees, exhausted. Although he was thin, he was heavy. Tall. His eye on one side was swollen, a gash deep on his forehead. There was no point offering him water. Nefyn listened to him breathing, the sound unfamiliar. Perhaps it was her tiredness but he looked at once completely real and entirely unreal. She had walked this way year after year. Sat in this boathouse time after time, and sharing it now seemed almost an impossibility. She got up and walked to the back of the boathouse. Here there were tools, her father's fishing nets. More lobster pots. She found a hurricane lamp, half filled with oil, and a tin matchbox, the kind that all fishermen favoured. She struck a match and let the strip of oil-soaked fabric light and push away the gloom around her.

It was darkening outside now and once more the repentant sea was calm. It would not go back to its former colour for a few days, as if its shame left a stain on it. She had often thought that it never truly did go back. That once a storm like that took place, things changed for ever. Nefyn brought the lamp back towards the boat, stepped inside and pulled the tarpaulin over herself, too. And as the soft light of the lamp illuminated them, they both lay in the broken boat under the unfeeling stars.

9

Boathouse • Marfa • Storfa

THAT MORNING NEFYN HAD placed her hand on his forehead. He still felt far away. Aching, she had pulled herself up and edged open the boathouse door. For the first time that she could remember, she turned her back to the sea and walked up the path to the cottage without searching the strandline. She drank some water, buttered some bread, ate and washed, the cuts on her arms and under her feet stinging in the lukewarm water. She pulled on a clean dress and the cardigan left for her, and set about collecting the specimens one after the other, placing them in an old shoebox. Then she started sweeping the floor, the shattered glass scratching the slabs beneath the broom.

As she worked, her mind was back in the boatshed. Perhaps it was the effect of the storm or her exertions in dragging his body up the beach, but she had slept deeply last night. A dark, dreamless sleep without the nightmares that usually plagued her. She had woken early as the curlews cried, listening to his breathing as a new day opened around them.

She leant the broom on the wall before going to count the tablets that were left on the kitchen sill. She hadn't taken any since Joseph had left but she calculated that he would be away at least another fourteen days. Perhaps the man would have gone by then and her brother needn't know anything about him.

The knock on the door caught her breath.

Nefyn's heart set to beating a chaotic rhythm, her throat tightened. She hurried into the kitchen, stepped behind the door, listened to the sound of the front door being pushed open.

'Nefyn? Nefyn, it's me.'

She had come in. Footsteps on broken glass. A silence. She held her breath. She could still sense her near. A moment. Then, the sound of Efa sweeping the last of the glass on the living-room floor. Nefyn stood, frozen, willing Efa anywhere else but here.

Her brother had always told her never to trust Efa. They needed her, yes, but Nefyn should never talk to her. Never confide in her. Never let her in. And they had argued, Joseph and Nefyn. Nefyn had always sensed Efa's loyalty, the attentions that would have petered out over the years if they had not been genuine. The slights and continued exclusion that Efa had endured should have given her ample excuse to desist, but Joseph was adamant.

Nefyn had watched Efa too, from afar. Followed her back from a distance in the summer when she came on foot, just to the outskirts of the village. Sat in the zinc shed by the front door looking out through the cracks in the panels, so she could get a closer look at her face, her clothes. Watched as she knocked and patiently waited, a certain expectation in her face that Nefyn had grown to feel sorry for.

Now Nefyn listened to her sweep the glass, her footsteps getting fainter as they moved towards the front door. Nefyn thought that she might leave, strained to hear, but then she was back again, standing in the middle of the living room, her hands clasped together. Pale face, a restlessness.

'Nefyn? Are you there? I didn't mean to frighten you. I just wanted to make sure you were all right.'

Efa stood waiting for an answer.

'Please, Nefyn? I worry about you.'

She started walking towards the kitchen. Nefyn's heart leapt.

'Stop,' she said instinctively. 'I'm all right.'

Efa stopped, Nefyn's voice startling her.

'Are you sure?'

Nefyn edged forward a little. Forcing herself to move. It was the only way to get rid of her. She inched her foot forward, pushed herself to lean until she stepped into the doorway, the light finding the redder shades in her hair. Efa gasped. Drank her in, like someone who had thirsted for a long time. She hadn't seen her face properly in so long, only her back, her hair. Glimpses. Efa smiled softly, Nefyn's face a reward in itself.

'It's like looking at your mother,' she said under her breath. Her eyes wandered, until she registered Nefyn's discomfort. She looked away, not wanting to cause her pain. 'I'm sorry,' she said, 'I can see you're well.' She moved to turn before looking up at her again as if knowing that this might be her only opportunity. 'I want you to know that coming to look after you is not . . . work for me . . .' She frowned. She shook her head, tilted it to make the words fall into place. 'That I have been glad to be a help.'

Nefyn noticed that her fingers wound around her coat buttons.

'That it has brought me a lot of joy.' Efa's face flushed, the words laid out bare between them. Nefyn studied her as Efa brought her senses back to the present. 'Right, well, then. I'll go now. You know where I am if you need me.' Efa smiled again, Nefyn's youth making her ache for her own. She turned to walk to the door.

'I didn't know you knew my mother.' Nefyn's words came despite herself. Efa stopped. Turned.

'Yes . . . she used to come to the church sometimes,' Efa chose her words carefully, 'when she needed to. I think she felt at peace there.'

The church was slowly being buried in the swirling dunes now, its ageing congregation dwindling. Long-buried memories stirred in Nefyn. Her mother's anger at the Church.

'I liked her very much,' Efa said again, 'and I can see that you're like her.'

Nefyn studied her and for the first time they stood, two women opposite each other, and Efa could feel time turning around them both. Efa smiled once more, and moved to leave.

Nefyn followed Efa to the door and stood for a moment, watching her go, a strange heaviness in her body, before the boathouse brought her back to the present.

Nefyn found the brandy her brother hid in his room and a hot-water bottle. She boiled the kettle and placed everything in a basket before hurrying down the path to the cove. She looked around once more. There would always be more people wandering the coast after a storm. It seemed to draw them. Bring them together as if nature's impetuousness, its unpredictability, was a common enemy. But there was no one visible. The cliff-tops empty. Perhaps it was too early. She slipped into the boatshed and waited as her eyes adjusted to the darkness. She stood, her pupils widening, her eyes scanning. The boat was empty. She put down the basket, walked slowly towards it. Listening. Her eyes straining. Then, she reached out for the corner of the tarpaulin and snatched it away. There was no one here. She stood, let out a disbelieving laugh. She had been seeing things. She must have been. A panic was starting to rise in her. Her brother was right. When in piques of frustration, he'd talk of her madness. This was proof. Her stomach clenched. Quivered.

'Who are you?'

The voice came from behind her. Faltering. Deep. She turned. He was clutching his side. His eyes scanning her face. Nefyn shook her head. His solidity. His animation startling.

'What happened?' he asked again. There was nothing but the sound of the sea.

'There was a storm,' Nefyn ventured. 'You came in on the tide.'

He tried to take in her words, studied her mouth trying to fathom what she was saying, but the pain was all-consuming. His eyes rolled and he coughed so violently he brought up sputum coloured pink with blood. Nefyn watched him in fear, crouched down, tipped out the contents of the basket and picked up the bottle of brandy. She offered it up to him.

'Please, take it.'

He looked at it.

'It will help with the pain.'

He nodded, gasping. She shakily unscrewed the cap and helped hold the bottle to his mouth. He gulped, the sting of spices filling his senses. Then he leant back against the door. He was breathing hard, his breast-bone concave. He drank some more, and as he did, she came into focus. His left eye still swollen, his vision unbalanced. She was thin, sullen-eyed. She was watching him steadily.

'I don't know what happened.' He pushed out the words through the pain.

Nefyn looked at him.

'I think you've broken your side . . . your ribs. You need to be careful. You need to rest.' Hamza listened to her voice as her face came in and out of focus. He hadn't known physical pain like it. Each breath an ordeal. A piercing, brilliant sliver of pain shooting to his lungs whenever he inhaled.

'Please, sit,' Nefyn said, watching the way the pain changed his breathing. He held out his arm behind him, lowered himself.

'These clothes . . .' he muttered.

'I'm sorry, you were wet, cold.' He nodded. Nefyn crouched, took some bread from the basket. Offered it to him.

'I don't know if you should eat? If you want to?' He shook his head. His eyes were glazing over now, his breathing becoming more laboured.

'Have you . . . have you anything . . .' he gasped, 'anything more for the pain?'

Nefyn shook her head and then remembered the tablets on the sill.

'Maybe,' she said, listening to the rasping of his lungs. 'I'll be back soon.'

He was unable to nod. He sat, immobile, as Nefyn pushed past him and ran back to the cottage through the thickening light.

10

Light ♦ Golau ♦ Daw'

EFA BUTTONED THE COAT under Emrys's chin. He looked smart. He always did. When it had started, she used to catch a glimpse of him across a room some-times, and forget that he was not the same any more. But now, his confusion had entered his body, too. In his uncertain gait. The way he stared a little too long in order to comprehend. She smiled at him, rubbed the sides of his arms with her palms. He could do with some fresh air.

The harbourside was busy, a stream of worried boat owners surveying the damage. Not fishermen – they were long gone – but the sons of fishermen, fiercely protective of the hobby dinghies, which, although rarely used, represented a part of themselves that they were unwilling to let go. Two men in yellow jackets were brushing the shale back into the water off the harbour walls. Redefining limits. Reinstating boundaries that had been blurred by the storm. Efa led Emrys to the café and sat him down before ordering some tea. A young girl with eyeliner too heavy for her perfect eyes took her order.

Although largely empty, the talk was of the road collapse to the north. The pictures in the paper. The Doctor. Efa had read the newspaper early this morn-ing. She had picked it up from the doormat, smoothed it out on the kitchen table. The instinct to go and tell

Emrys the news had started to fade. Emrys had known him, they both had.

The Doctor had been the one who gently asked Emrys those first questions. He had known to come to the house of course, supposedly for a cup of tea, knowing that Emrys would not come to the surgery to see him. Efa had set about boiling the kettle, all the while consumed with guilt that for the first time in over fifty years, she was complicit with another man behind her husband's back. The Doctor asked him about the year. The time. Efa tried not to react as Emrys digressed, avoided the answers, left strange pauses in the middle of his speech. A few weeks later, Efa sat in the Doctor's office, handbag in her lap as he kindly confirmed her suspicions. He had expressed sympathy not with words, but with silence. She said that they had had a good life together. Many years of happiness. He answered that it was human nature, that however much happiness we've had, we yearn for more. He would help her weather the storm.

Efa had gone upstairs and sat on their bed this morning. Emrys had looked at her blankly and stroked her back gently, feeling that something was amiss with his wife.

Efa smiled as the young girl brought over their tea, set it down absent-mindedly. There would be a public funeral, they said. Once the body was released. It was a pity, added one. A great pity, but they consoled themselves that he had had a good life. Wasn't it strange? And just like that, the swell of their conversation stopped and they went back to their breakfasts. Emrys was looking at her. She smiled, reached out to touch the side of his face and whispered, 'Come on now, drink your tea before it gets cold.'

∽

Hamza had felt his whole body loosen, the brandy and the tranquillizer combining in a blissful oblivion. He had drowned. He was sure of it. He remembered the dark, the world collapsing beneath them. Flashes of the Doctor's pale face and the noise. Deafening. Howling. And then he had swum. Willing his numb arms, his heavy legs, as the water's iciness seeped into his every pore. It was so dark that air and water were the same colour. Both smothering. And in the darkness dawned faces in his mind: his wife, his mother, his brother, his son. Up and down they turned and then disappeared. And as he slipped further away from his body, he felt a release. His father was there again. His voice under the fierce sun: 'Let go! Don't fight! Let go!' Hamza had felt the life drain from his numb hands. Could not feel his legs, his heat flooding to his heart. He could not breathe the air, it wasn't enough – what about breathing water? The thought had slid into his mind so easily, so effortlessly. The simple serenity that the thought brought him. The blessed feeling of the interchange of air and water, water and air. Over and over again in an unending cycle of life and death. And then, the quiet. The offering up of oneself. The peace.

Hamza lay for a moment in the broken boat and breathed. Watching his chest rise and fall. Stubbornly, relentlessly, confounding everything he remembered, the daylight a sharp triangle on his chest through the chink in the door. He lifted his fingers and let them glow in its luminosity. Stunningly beautiful. He smiled, pulled himself up, stumbled towards the door, and edged it open. His eyes narrowed. The salt in the air. The nonchalant sea. He sat in the doorway looking out for a moment, breathing properly for the first time in years.

Up at the house, Nefyn scraped the ashes from the fireplace. He'd need to be kept warm. She bundled the kindling into the grate, pushed it back. The wind was coming from the sea today, drawing the chimney. She had watched him sleep last night. Almost newborn. The swelling in his eye had eased, allowing her to see the symmetry of his face for the first time. Dark eyes, angled cheekbones. Middle-aged. His skin peeling slightly from having been in the water. Clearing Joseph's room, she had placed more clean clothes out for him. Cooked some broth her mother used to make. There was an urgency in her preparations. He would be safer here. She looked across to the window. It would be getting dark soon. He was so unsure on his feet still that moving him in the complete darkness would be dangerous. She had not given him another tablet today, so he would be in more pain, but that would be preferable to him being unable to navigate the treacherous path from the cove to the cottage. She must go down.

She found him asleep, his head resting against the open boatshed door, his face serene. She stood, looking at him for a moment, before kneeling. Touching his arm gently.

'Wake up, come . . . come with me.'

His confused eyes took her in warily but his weakness made him compliant. He pulled himself up on the doorframe, leant on to her thin shoulders. Nefyn felt his weight skew her centre of gravity. They walked slowly towards the foot of the path. When it came into view, he shook his head.

'No . . . no. It's impossible. Please.'

She looked up at him through the half-light.

'No, it isn't, nothing is impossible.'

He looked at her, the pain gnawing at his insides, but there was something in the steadiness of her face that made him trust her.

'Come on.' She pulled at him and they started their slow and painful ascent.

They had barely reached the cottage when the team of searchers rounded Porth y Wrach in their dinghy. They came ashore determined to comb the beach and cove one more time before the light died. They walked in a perfect line across the shingle. One officer came to the boathouse, pulled at the door and looked in, but it was dark. Nothing but an old boat. The smell of oil. Dampness. The others shouted at him. They were finished for the night. He turned, walked towards them, not seeing Hamza's old clothes strewn across the boatshed floor.

11

Fire • Tân • Hariq

NEFYN ALLOWED HIS WEIGHT to fall back on to the chair by the fire. The cottage was cold, its stones and slates hard to heat, but the fire was better than nothing. She wrapped a blanket around his shoulders and stepped back, unsure what to do next. His temples were damp with sweat, his chest labouring. She stood, feeling the heat of his body against hers dissipate into the cold room. Waiting to see if his breathing would settle before fetching him another tablet.

He looked up at her face as she offered it to him, took it and pressed it to his mouth, swallowing the tablet whole. She offered him water but he just hung his head. She waited, watching. Listened to his breathing and the fire gaining strength.

'Who lives here with you?' he asked eventually.

'My brother, but he's away fishing.' Her voice was small. Her breathing shallow. He looked up at her.

'Did you tell anyone about me?'

Nefyn shook her head and thought she saw his shoulders drop imperceptibly.

'I'm sorry,' he mumbled again. His breathing becoming more ragged. He studied her face, the stillness in it.

'This makes no sense. I shouldn't be here . . . I . . .' His words failed him once again. 'I was a prisoner at the base. The military base – you know it?'

Nefyn nodded.

'How far is it? How far from here?' he asked.

'Not far.' She shrugged. 'Maybe five miles.'

He nodded.

'There was an accident. They were trying to move me . . . I was in the water.'

He started coughing again. Nefyn waited for it to ease.

'Do you have a phone I could use?' Nefyn shook her head, her green eyes troubled. Hamza nodded.

'Listen . . . you've done so much for me.' He laughed. 'I don't know who . . . maybe God, maybe . . .' he tailed off. He shook his head, his thoughts muddled. 'But if you can find it in your heart to trust me, not tell anyone I am here.'

She was looking at him now, her eyes darkening.

'I understand if you can't . . . but if you could . . .'

Nefyn thought for a moment about who she could tell. A silence fell between them as he awaited her response.

'Will you help me?' he asked again.

She was difficult to read, her face at once closed and accepting. There were no questions. No asking for details. It was as if she had been expecting him. Finally, Nefyn nodded. His shoulders dropped.

'I'm Hamza. My name is Hamza.'

Nefyn repeated the name in her head.

'Nefyn,' she said.

They studied each other a moment. Then she nodded simply.

'I've made you some food.'

*

63

Hamza watched her go, feeling the warmth of the fire starting to reach his bones. The room was dark, heavy. Firewood stacked along the chimney breast, empty glass cabinets. Aged oak furniture. Driftwood on the window-sills. And some old maps of the sea hung under the low ceilings. Hamza's eyes were instinctively drawn to them. He could hear Nefyn moving dishes in the kitchen. The older maps with their sinewy lines, illustrated with wrecks and sea monsters. They glowed in the firelight. She returned, two bowls of soup in her hands. She placed one in his lap, put the spoon in his right hand, made sure he could lift the spoon to his mouth before she sat on a low stool opposite him. They ate, listening to the fire.

'This is good,' he said, his voice weak.

Nefyn nodded. The sound of their spoons on the crockery. Hamza watched her for a moment, put down his spoon. Waited for the words to come to him. 'My grandfather was a fisherman too.' Nefyn listened, the light of the fire warming the tone of her skin. 'He had maps, of the sea.' Nefyn followed his gaze, turned her head to look behind her at the maps. Looked back at him. 'He would let me look at them when I was a child. Old ones, from when people really used them to try and understand the world.' He swallowed, each word painful. 'He showed me portolan charts of the sea . . . the clay maps of Iraq.' His face softened and Nefyn smiled. 'I really loved them . . . there was wonder in them. So much possibility.'

Nefyn watched him, waited for him to continue but he didn't. He closed his eyes, a shadow coming across his face. Nefyn put down her bowl, her spoon clattering. She got to her feet, slid her arm under his.

'Come,' she said gently. 'You need to rest.'

His words had left him. Worn away by his tiredness and the loss of adrenaline. He leant on Nefyn, feeling again the bones of her shoulders through her dress. 'This way,' she said, leading him to Joseph's room. There, she sat him on the bed, removed his shoes and laid him down on his side. She knelt, her hand on the edge of his ribcage. Counting his breaths until he had settled into sleep. Then, she took him in once again. The dark curls matted with salt, the curve of his earlobe down to his jaw. She hadn't been so close to someone apart from her brother in so long. Her father, she remembered, was shorter, his skin sea-weathered, his hands rope-roughened and hard. Joseph was different, reddish hair the colour of sea pine. She listened to him for a moment longer before getting to her feet and closing the door gently. She moved towards the fire, loaded on some more wood to keep it burning through the night, and looked up at the old maps, luminous in the golden light.

12

Dunes ✦ Twyni ✦ Kuthban

THE LIEUTENANT COLONEL KNOTTED his tie in front of the mirror. He was wearing full dress uniform today. The car would pick him up at noon. He could count on one hand the number of times when it had been necessary to cross out of the base into the village, but they had to be seen at the Doctor's funeral. He had, after all, given the base many years of faithful service. They had taken advice from their public relations officers, and they had agreed: they did not want to draw attention to the fact that the incident occurred on army operations, but they didn't want to risk being conspicuous by their absence either. They would cover the funeral costs of course, out of courtesy, but they'd been at pains to point out to the Doctor's widow that the accident had been an unfortunate act of God. That the Doctor, having attended to a soldier at the base, returned to his car to find that the engine would not turn over. He had accepted a lift back to the village on a truck going that way with supplies, and it was so terrible that it was at that moment the storm had hit, and the cliff road had fallen away.

He straightened his tie and noticed that he had nicked himself whilst shaving that morning. He swore under his breath and licked his finger to rub away the blood from his immaculate collar.

He had taken a walk once, when he was first posted

here, to get the literal lie of the land. He'd looked down at the village. The backwaters. Thought about how it would be possible to live there, die there, completely unseen. Living a life, speaking a near-dead language that no one cared about. Voiceless. The thought had led him to gather his coat about him and turn back for the barracks. They were all living in blissful ignorance of the realities of the world, sleeping, like children. The drones tested on their waters a part of an ongoing conflict of surveillance and covert operations. Taking out targets thousands of miles away, discreetly, cleanly, meant that they could be at war without declaring war. It was all rather civilized. He picked up his hat. There came a knock at the door.

'The car's here, sir.'

'Of course.'

He walked the corridor, his patent shoes creaking. The Captain held the door open for him, went around the car and got in himself.

'Any news?' he asked, his voice tight under his collar.

'Nothing yet, sir, there seems to be no sign.'

The driver turned the engine over.

'Has General Reeves called again?'

'I'm afraid so, sir.'

The Lieutenant Colonel took this in.

'Why on earth hasn't his body washed in by now?'

The Captain sat in silence for a moment. Let his senior consider his own frustration.

'Perhaps we'll need to do some discreet house-to-house. Just to make sure.'

The Captain nodded.

'Yes, sir.'

'Get the police to do it.'

'Of course.'

'Keep some distance.'

'Yes, sir.'

He tapped the window and the driver pulled away. He sat back, adjusted his gloves.

'Now, let's get this over with.'

Efa stuffed the colourful scarf into the pocket of her black coat. Emrys would become troubled when he saw her dressed head-to-toe in black; deep down somewhere he would be aware of the association. So, Efa would wear a bright scarf around her neck whenever she left the house for a funeral. Their next-door neighbour, Mary, who liked to think of herself as a charitable type, would come over sometimes to care for Emrys. She would help him dress, sit with him as he stared out of the window, her pen scratching words in her puzzle book. Her patience, though, would sometimes wear thin, so Efa would make sure to heap praise on her, tell her often that she didn't know what she'd do without her. Bring her a little something. Then, all would be well again, until the next time. In this way, Efa could continue looking after the houses, keep adding to their pension, which would make all the difference. If she finished her work early, she could also go to the café and take a cup of tea alone. Looking out at the sea. Feeling her back ache with the washing, the caring and the dressing.

The church was full, as Efa had expected, so she had to stand at the back. There were only ten pews each side anyway, a wooden cross and the shadows of ancient paintings haunting damp walls. After high winds, the warden would have to sweep the sand out through the vestibule, the shifting dunes outside threatening to engulf the place of worship.

Efa remembered the families that owned the pews. How they would sit in the same ones each Sunday. Now, there was no such order. She remembered the funerals of fishermen, their coffins draped in nets, the prayers said for the drowned. As children, they were free to roam around the dunes as their parents prayed. In winter the dunes remained eerily silent, nothing but the sound of the wind in the reeds. But in summer, lizards and adders would lie lazily in the sun, whilst dark green fritillary and gatekeeper butterflies vied for space with scarlet tiger and Portland moths. She would lie listening to the hymns, the dunes ablaze around her. And once, she remembered running, following the jagged flight of a butterfly after a summer storm, and how having lost its trail she found herself standing in the wind-whipped graveyard, the sand having dissipated and shifted, revealing broken coffins and bones. She remembered standing amongst the exposed remains, her hair blowing in the wind, and knowing deep down that nobody really truly disappeared.

The mourners were mostly from the village today. The Doctor's family. One or two in military uniform, a nod to his long service at the base. His wife was brought in on the arms of her sons to a respectful hush, her face achingly white against her black dress. The service was brief. Hymns sung without music and an invitation extended to everyone present to take tea at the church hall, which the military had kindly offered to pay for. Efa would have to be getting back.

As was tradition, the Doctor's wife stood, exhausted, on the way out of the church, greeting each mourner. She was flanked by her worried-looking sons. Efa held her hand, touched her cheek with hers, told her what a good man her husband had been. Knew from the stunned look on her face that she would remember none of it. The church had soon warmed up with the heat of tears and candles and life so that now, as she walked out into the day, Efa felt the bitter wind knifing through her. She reached into her pocket and wrapped the colourful scarf around her, trying desperately to shrug off the cold.

Watching her go was a young man, fair-haired, shielding a cigarette from the wind in order to light it. He inhaled. His eyes narrow. He'd heard the talk in the NAAFI. Heard how they'd dragged three bodies from the sea. He watched as the two senior officers walked back to their black car, his eyes boring into the back of the tallest. He exhaled, flicked the ash away into the sand and wondered where they were hiding the fourth.

13

Hikaaya • Stori • Story

S HE HEARD HIM TALKING first, in his sleep. An agitation to his voice. Asking something she did not understand. Then came a creak and footsteps on the wooden floor. Heavy, purposeful, shocking. She had lain still, fear prickling through her. She steadied her breath. The sound of walking. Abrupt stopping. Laughing. Poltergeist in the dark. She pushed away the covers and walked to her door, eased it open quietly.

He was on his knees, praying now. Not praying, perhaps. Surveying something. His dark eyes wide open. Nefyn watched him, held her breath. He pulled at something on the floor, his nails scraping the boards. He didn't look in her direction. And then the placing of his hands began. On the floor, in front of him, above him, as if he couldn't fathom his reality, his palms jarring against invisible walls. His face pale in the moonlight. A translucent barrier, a wall of air around him, pressing in on him – she could see that – his breathing becoming shallower. The placing of hands on himself, his face, his neck. Over and over. He wasn't talking now either; there were just sounds, as if language had left him. Dh. Gh. Sh. Each offering painful to the ear. He wasn't there, had left himself in the dark. A shell.

She knew she could not wake him, that it would frighten him, that she could only watch, witness his body speak. The placing continued over and over, testing the air until he got up, abruptly. Nefyn watched, the cold night tightening her skin. He walked towards her, purposefully. Nefyn froze. He stood, his face inches from hers, studying her. His breath on her face. Muttering. But she was invisible. She listened to him, her heart beating heavily, his voice whispering like the winds.

He moved past her towards the fireplace. He was looking for something. Calling. A desperation in his voice. It sounded like a name. Hassan? Hussein? Perhaps. The name didn't come from his mouth, but from somewhere else. Somewhere deeper. It echoed within him. Over and over he asked. Until his body was merely a vessel. He took the blankets from the chairs and scattered them on the floor. The name filled every part of him until, eventually, his voice grew weaker. At last, he was silent. She watched him stand, his shoulders sunken, his chest concave. Exhausted. His hands empty. She waited. Then, slowly, she approached him, slid her hand into his. Felt his senses registering her. He was cold. She pulled him gently, guided him back towards his rest.

Nefyn watched over him in the dark. Waited for his breathing to settle. It had been warmer the last few days, and the air had slid on to the sea, condensing into a thick fog. The world would not be visible in the morning. It was unlike the fogs that formed over land, thin and fickle, moved on by winds. This fog was heavy, lipid almost, stuck to the insides of the lungs, clung damply to clothes. It smothered sounds, made you seek deeper breaths.

Hamza woke before dawn. Not a physical awakening but a return to the self. As consciousness slid back into his eyes, she brought him black tea, with plenty of sugar. His body ached, his throat. She left him to drink and started to relight the fire. It wasn't dawn yet, though some of the birds were trying to mark their presence through the fog. He watched the steam from his mug curling into the cold air. Shakily, he walked barefoot towards her. Sat by the hearth. She was offering a lit match to the expired tinder, waiting for it to catch hold once again.

'My throat is sore,' he said at last. Nefyn smiled, replaced the matches. Piled some dry wood on to the flame. Blew on it to strengthen it.

'You were calling for someone – Hussein?' she said gently. Hamza looked at her in confusion. 'In your sleep.' She placed her hands around her legs. Rested her chin on her knees. Waited for the fire to take hold.

'I'm sorry, I . . .'

'There's no need.'

'There are so many things . . .' he tried to explain. He tried to think of something to tell her. Of home. But the fragmented words were ruins in his mouth. 'It has been nine years since I have been home.' Nefyn thought about this. Could not imagine it. 'I hate it.' Nefyn pulled her cardigan around her. Listened. 'War. It takes away so many ways of talking about home. It smothers everything. People think it's the fighting, but it's more than that. The horror is gentler than that. It dominates stories. Rubs out tradition, kindness, joy, makes people's lives invisible.' Hamza stopped. Drew a long breath.

'Have you always lived here?' he asked. Nefyn nodded.

'I was born here, in this cottage,' she smiled. 'I've never left the cove.'

Hamza smiled, looked at her. Her seeming isolation. Questions stirred inside him but he did not take the liberty of asking them. She looked away again. There was something of the tide about her. Sometimes somehow close, within his grasp, but at others slipping away. They sat in silence for a moment.

Nefyn got up, suddenly preoccupied, and reached for the box that she had placed the specimens in. Pulled it into her lap. Looked up uncertainly before opening it. She picked up a transparent by-the-wind sailor, smiled softly, and handed it to him. He took its exquisite form in his fingers. Let his pupils widen and focus.

'You collect things?'

Nefyn nodded.

They spent the day looking through the objects, one by one. Holding them between them: shells, herring-gull skulls, brittle stars and egg cases split and gaping. Delicate. Fragile. Lit from within. Nefyn explained them to him, their shapes, colours, structures. Their infinite variety and the way they adapted in order to survive. The way the molluscs built their shells around them, layer by layer, day by day, and the wonder that they shared common patterns. Hamza smiled, listened. Her face became animated as she held each object like words that had washed ashore, the fragments of a story of which she was determined to make sense.

And then, when the day was dulling, Nefyn filled

a bowl with hot water and soap and carried it through to the living room, placed it on a low table which she dragged across the flagstones towards her. He was staring at the fire now, unsure whether he was awake or not, the day folding in on itself around them. Nefyn placed a towel around his shoulders, and pulled his head gently backwards. The water steamed in the cold air as Nefyn began to wash his hair. Unhurriedly, silently. Its matted saltiness relaxed by the water into stubborn curls. Hamza felt the water, warm on his scalp, and was stunned into silence by the gentleness of her touch. A quiet absolution. His vision blurred, and tears fell darkly down his cheeks, but he didn't move to rub them away. Nefyn saw but did not react, continued to rub the blood that had dried hard and black on his forehead. She rinsed the flannel in the bowl over and over and watched the water cloud with old blood. When she had finished, she dried his face gently, tucked the towel into his collar and pulled his chair closer to the fire so he could keep warm.

14

Host • Mudif • Gwesteiwr

THE LIEUTENANT COLONEL SAT at his desk and waited, wanting to be in situ when Owens arrived. He had spent a considerable time thinking about the different ways in which to handle the guard. He could let things slide, of course, but knowing his character, he would exploit this as a weakness and push the boundaries further. He had no proof that Owens had indeed beaten the prisoner and the fact that Adley was now dead complicated the matter.

However, the advantage he had over him was information. He had studied Owens's record. Flicked through his file. He was from a council estate. Joined at sixteen. Excelled at the physical side of things and was eager to learn. His only weakness, it seemed, was an unwillingness to let things go. In the Lieutenant Colonel's experience it was often men who'd never seen active service who treated prisoners badly. Those who had been on the front line usually respected their prisoners more, knowing that one day their fates could well be reversed.

Unbeknownst to Owens, he and the Lieutenant Colonel were not as different as it might seem. He had shared the same upbringing. The same comprehensive schools. The Lieutenant Colonel's father would make him fight with his brothers in order to toughen him up. Being the youngest, he never came out of it well. He had evened out his accent by now, but he knew it was still there, at gala dinners, in the exclusion from certain clubs, in the way he envied others' social ease. And in the bad drafts to isolated outposts, like this one. When General Reeves had first suggested he oversee the testing, he had emphasized how sensitive the site was and how grateful he'd be if the Lieutenant Colonel would consider it. Flattered, he had accepted, but as the years rolled by, he had come to realize that it was in all senses an outpost. A grinding, thankless task. He had done his time in the backwaters and with the end of the testing came the prospect of a new appointment. His wife, steadfast in her support of him over the years, was eager to leave too. She could bear the bland Chief Officer's house, with its beige walls and serving hatch, much better when there were more distractions near by. A town of some sort, a city even. When the children were small, she had been preoccupied with them, but they had gone their own ways now, and her patience had begun to wear thin. The exchanges between them had always been layered, him never saying what he meant, the military euphemisms woven into the fabric of their marriage. But she had finally said, recently, that she wasn't happy. And he could feel it in her silences, her distracted tone, her listlessness.

There had been other challenges. One drone was lost at sea, another came down near a school, but it was nothing that some newly donated equipment couldn't fix. The drones were unmanned, but that didn't mean that they were unpiloted. Guided by men prone to human error. They had tried to minimize the 'humanity' of the operation, studying data, creating algorithms, but people had a natural propensity for the chaotic, the unpredictable, which made their calculations difficult. Human error was inevitable, the occasional mistake, but there was something entirely different about the behaviour of this soldier Owens, a wilfulness that he found singularly unappealing. The silent vehemence that seeped from him.

They wouldn't 'host' prisoners often, having neither the facilities nor the capacity, but they would occasionally pass through on the request of General Reeves. It was often about delay tactics. The keeping and moving of a prisoner over a period of time could bury the problem. Make those who cared forget. The Lieutenant Colonel had assured Reeves a few days ago that the prisoner's body, when found, would disappear. That the matter was all in hand.

It was difficult for the gatekeepers, the officers in daily contact with the prisoners, so they profiled them, selected the most exemplary. It was unusual to have such a disciplined grassroots man as Owens have such independence of thought. He lit a cigarette. Leant back on his chair. He could hear him coming. He inhaled deeply and rested the cigarette in the ashtray. Narrowed his eyes as the knock came.

'Enter.'

He had decided not to let him sit. He watched him come in, close the door behind him. He picked up the cigarette once again, inhaled. Took his time. Let him stand until he was ready to speak.

'Your conduct was irresponsible. You could have killed him.'

Owens smiled. 'It was nothing to do with me,' he said, his voice controlled, 'it was all Adley.'

The Lieutenant Colonel fixed a steady gaze on him. 'Was it, now?'

'And anyway, I think you'll find that it's you who's managed to kill him,' he answered.

The Lieutenant Colonel let the words hang between them. 'If you think that you could expose this and be believed, you're very much mistaken.'

Owens squared his shoulders. The Lieutenant Colonel regarded him. Didn't hurry.

'I have your record here.' Owens's smile faltered. The Lieutenant Colonel retrieved the new file he had compiled from the drawer of the desk. Flicked it open. Took his time. 'I think you'll find that you're not very well liked amongst your colleagues. There have been a few . . . misdemeanours.' Owens scoffed. The Lieutenant Colonel looked up sharply. 'I don't know what's so funny.'

'I have nothing on my file.'

'That's strange, because according to this you do . . . assault . . . failing to report for duty . . . sailed quite close to the wind on several occasions.'

'Those are lies.'

'Are you saying I'm seeing things? It's right here in black and white.' He pushed the file towards him. Owens refused to look down. 'The thing is, Prisoner B was a figment of your imagination. What proof have you got that he even existed?'

'You can't do that.'

'Can't I?' The Lieutenant Colonel closed the file. Steadied his voice.

'What about the Doctor?'

'He's not going to speak now, is he? Neither is your friend Adley. Now ...' The Lieutenant Colonel leant forward, intertwined his fingers. 'Here is how this is going to work. You will carry on with your duties as usual. Forget about everything. And who knows? Maybe your record will improve. Or you can make this difficult for yourself, and with your little file here, you wouldn't be doing yourself any favours. If I flag any of these "infringements", you'll be on your way to Colchester for a little holiday.' The Lieutenant Colonel observed him coolly. Owens had clenched his fists unconsciously, his jaw setting. 'Now, I think you'll agree with me that this matter is closed.'

The younger man's neck was flushed with anger. He turned, walked towards the door.

'And one more thing,' said the Lieutenant Colonel. Owens paused, did not turn around. 'Don't you ever speak to me like that again.'

15

Chwedl • *Myth* • *Khurafa*

HAMZA SLEPT FOR A day and a half. Nefyn had done nothing but tend the fire and watch over him. The bruising on his side was yellowing. His breathing was growing a little more even, deeper, as if the pain from his ribs was no longer catching as he inhaled. He had slept silently, this time. So much so that she had gone to him and pressed her hand on his chest to check his breathing every now and then. When he woke, she had re-warmed some mutton stew for him, guided him to the kitchen table. She observed him as he moved, noticed that the pain wasn't touching his face as much.

The rest had strengthened him and he had started to think about how he could leave here, his mind opening up painfully to the possibility of life. But whenever he tried to envisage it, his thoughts would cloud with fatigue. He was only five miles from the military base, and they would be looking for him. If he left here, he'd be caught. There was no phone. When he had first been captured, he had fantasized about what he would do if he managed to get away, but he could not have envisioned this. He had some family in France. They could help him, perhaps. They could contact his brother, if he was alive. The logistics he would have to work out, but he was troubled, too, about relying more on Nefyn. He watched as she made more tea, poured fresh water into the kettle. Her eyes alighting on the row of white tablets on the windowsill. His eyes followed hers uneasily.

'I'm worried I have been taking your medication.' Nefyn looked back at him. Said nothing. 'Those pills, they are for you?'

'Yes.'

'I'm sorry, I don't want you to get sick.'

Nefyn smiled. 'I won't.'

Hamza shifted his weight carefully, his brow furrowing.

'But the doctor gave them to you?'

'My brother gives them to me,' she said. Hamza studied her as she took down two cups.

'But they're for pain? Yes? What happens if you don't take them?'

Nefyn thought for a moment. Put the cups on the table. 'I . . . I feel things . . .' Hamza smiled. She shrugged.

'What kind of things?'

'I feel more of things . . . the things that other people feel.'

'But maybe that's good?'

Nefyn shook her head. 'I think it frightens him sometimes.' Her eyes were darkening now.

'And what about you?' he asked.

'It frightens me when I can't feel anything.'

Hamza felt a heaviness in his stomach.

'He doesn't want me to hurt,' said Nefyn again.

'I understand.'

'It's not his fault.'

Hamza studied her. He had been trying to pinpoint exactly what was different about her. Perhaps it was a stillness. Her acceptance. He couldn't quite find the words for it. She sat down opposite him. He looked at her for a while. Considered whether to confide in her, but the words came anyway.

'That name ... The name you heard me calling. Hussein.' He studied the rim of the cup for a moment, pressed his thumbnail into it. 'Hussein is my son,' he said simply. He dug up the name as if from soil. Brushed it clean. Nefyn nodded.

'And he's at home?' she asked.

Hamza's eyes flittered.

'I don't know.' His voice was heavy, translucent with tears. 'He was only a boy when ... He would be fourteen now. Nearly a man.' He stopped for a moment. Hamza looked down. 'Don't you see? I have lost him anyway.' Nefyn's face became troubled. 'Perhaps, coming back to life ... perhaps it is too hard.' Nefyn studied his face silently. Hamza smiled. 'When we first met, you said that nothing is impossible, but ...'

The fog still clung to the cottage. Thick and stubborn. Enclosing it in greyness. Time seemed erased by the lack of clarity between night and day. Each sleep ending when it needed to. Each day.

'You know, my wife, she used to tell him, "Go ask your father about his maps." It was her way of letting me know to keep him out of her way for a while.' Nefyn smiled. 'I would pull him into my lap, bury my face in his hair and tell him stories. Hold him, his skin on my cheek ... burning me almost, he was so alive to me.'

Nefyn watched as he saw his son in his mind's eye. 'Now it feels almost impossible that he exists. A young man. Strong. Broad shoulders. Perhaps he has a beard.' He laughed. 'The beginnings of a beard.' Hamza shook his head. Thought for a moment. 'His life seems more impossible than death. And in my mind, I am still holding him in my lap. Whispering stories to him.'

Nefyn's eyes widened.

'Sometimes a story is enough,' she said.

Hamza looked at her, let the silence between them grow. She began again uncertainly.

'My mother. When I was a girl . . .' She was cupping the tea with her hands now. She looked up again, searched his face for something and, having found it, said, 'She used to tell me a story. She said that she was different. She said that she came from the sea.' She waited for his expression to change, but it didn't. 'She was *of* the sea.'

'Atargatis,' Hamza said. She looked at him, puzzled. 'She was an ancient goddess from my country,' he explained. Nefyn smiled and continued.

'My father, he was fishing and he caught her in his net one day by Porth y Wrach. It's a stone arch on the headland. She was stolen. Taken. He kept her in this house. Wanted her to love him but she didn't. He forced her . . . and women of the sea, they always have twins. Two children. Together. One boy. One girl. Every time.'

'Like your brother and you?'

Nefyn nodded. 'She had a cloak; when he caught her, he hid it. She could never leave him without it. But one day, we came home. She was gone.'

'She found it?'

'She had spent her whole time here looking for it. Looking for a way to get away. Knowing that although she loved us, she didn't belong. We never saw her again.'

Hamza waited for the words to fall between them.

'So, you belong to the sea like your mother?' he asked. Nefyn shook her head.

'My father was from the land, my mother from the sea. Do you see? I'm trapped.'

Hamza thought of all the half-lives he had seen.

'Yes, I do,' he said. They sat in silence for a moment. 'It's a good story,' he said quietly. Nefyn looked at him and felt something change.

'Yes,' she said, 'yes, it is.'

16

Adre ♦ Home ♦ Bayt

JOSEPH HAD BEEN LYING with the girl in her bed when the storm hit the coast. She had been talking and he had stopped listening. She had lit like a struck match, her anger flaming, and turned her back on him until he placed his hand on her hip, tugged her towards him. Pressed some words into her ear. They had kissed again, angrily, and then, softening, she had climbed on top of him. Afterwards, he had lain listening to the wind around the small house and had thought of Nefyn and how all this would go. The girls that would show an interest in him, the nights he would share with them and then the inevitable questions. It was at this point that Joseph would turn in on himself and wait for the crying to start. Their frustration growing more heated the more he locked them out. His desire cooling further.

He had risen early, packed his things and worked for a day or two out of the harbour doing odd jobs, helping with the clear-up after the storm. But as the storm had kept boats in the harbour, and setting out fishing now would add a few more weeks, his mind turned back to Nefyn and the cove.

He had made the three-hour journey for years, watched as the flat coastal areas of the North rose to peaks in the mountains, pushed by the sea into impossible folds. Suffocating and protecting the villages in their embrace. The way the hills then modulated into open valleys of grasslands, fertile, water-riven, watched over by red kites until the soil grew pale again as he neared the coast and the salt marshes began tangling the waterfront. Each place subtly distinct, in moth and bird and dialect. Some drivers with whom he hitch-hiked expected him to talk, wanted him to alleviate their boredom. Expected it as payment for picking him up, but most of the time Joseph preferred to sit staring out of the window, allowing the hum of the engine to numb his mind. Shaking the rocking back-and-forth motion of the boats out of his system. The gruff orders, the smell of diesel, the stunned look of dead fish.

This morning, he sat, his backpack in his lap, sullen in his seatbelt. The lorry driver had switched on his radio. A subtle release from talking. He had picked up some more tablets from his contact on the way home, and some books. He felt their sharp angles through the canvas of his bag. When there had been a library in the village, he would exchange them for her, but now he would pick them up in second-hand shops here and there. She would almost snatch them from him, before disappearing to her room.

She had been right about the storm. Her warning to him. It had been weighing on his mind. His unease and guilt growing as he neared home. Their mother had always charged them with looking after each other. Had made him promise, the day before she left them. And he had, he had tried. Tried to keep her hidden, but they were barely more than children and he had made mistakes. He remembered the time that they had been playing on the beach, and he had run up to the cottage for his fishing rod. On his return, a group of young boys had encircled her. Caught her out in the open. They were laughing, goading, one boy pulling at her dress. He remembered dropping his rod and running as she screamed. Her hands over her ears. Her hair around her face. Prey. They were barely more than children, but he could have killed them. He almost did kill one of them, just to make sure they never came back to the cove.

The driver slowed, left the engine running and nodded as Joseph climbed down to the road, swung the heavy door shut. He walked towards the coast through the dunes, following the wooden walkways overgrown by reeds and ragworts. Walkways that were a gentle reminder of how difficult this terrain was on foot. He would not go back north for a while. He needed to let the dust settle on his argument with the girl. He rounded the bend to see the cottage, clinging stubbornly to the cliff. He knew Nefyn wouldn't have been frightened of the storm, but there was something about them that agitated her. He listened to the wind as it combed the reeds before walking on.

'Nefyn?'

Nefyn lay on her bed. Her eyes snapped open. Then, Hamza's voice, soft with alarm.

'Nefyn!' Joseph shouted again.

A scuffle. Nefyn jumped upright. Ran to open her bedroom door to find Hamza held by his collar against the doorframe. Joseph's face incandescent with fear and rage.

'It's all right! It's all right!' she cried.

'Who the hell are you? What have you done to her?'

Nefyn pulled at his arm.

'What are you doing here?! Joseph! What are you doing here?! Leave him. He's a friend. Leave him!' Joseph's eyes darted uncertainly towards Nefyn's face. He was breathing heavily. 'Please! Just listen. I didn't think you'd be back!' Nefyn pulled at his arm again. 'Let him go!'

Joseph shoved Hamza backwards, ripping his collar. His breathing heavy. His agitation twitching in his arm muscles. Hamza held his hands open, submissive.

'I'm sorry,' Hamza said.

'Where's he from?' barked Joseph. 'What's he doing here? These clothes . . . they're mine!'

'He's my friend,' Nefyn said, trying to steady Joseph's eyes on her.

'You don't have any friends,' Joseph shot back.

'He came from the beach.'

Joseph's eyes searched Nefyn's face in disbelief, the only sound that of his ragged breathing.

'What are you talking about?'

Hamza watched them, tried to appear small. Unthreatening.

'He was hurt, I've been nursing him.'

'But what does he want?'

'Nothing, he just needs to get better.'

'There are hospitals for that.'

'No. Nobody can know he's here.'

Joseph shook his head in disbelief.

'Please, I know this is difficult. I'm from Syria, I was being held, I just need to get home.'

'Who knows he's here?' Joseph asked again, his mind turning.

'No one.'

'They'll be looking for him, Nefyn. What does he know?'

'Nothing!' Nefyn stepped nearer to him, lowered her voice. Placed her hand on his arm. 'Please, Joseph.'

'No! This is none of our business. If they come here . . . We don't need them coming here, Nefyn.'

'We have to help him.'

'No.'

'Let me help him, Joseph!'

Hamza looked at her. Studied her face. She was oblivious to his eyes. Joseph rounded on her, grabbed her by the forearms. Hamza stepped forwards instinctively. Joseph's voice was tight now, threatening.

'Why won't you listen? You haven't been taking them, have you?'

Nefyn looked away. He jerked her arms. Demanded her attention.

'Look at me, Nefyn.' Her eyes fell to the floor. Joseph let her go roughly. He turned towards Hamza.

'I'm sorry for whatever's happened to you, but we can't help you.'

Hamza turned to Nefyn. She looked smaller now next to her brother.

'Go and pack your things,' Joseph said. 'Whatever you have. I'll give you some money.'

Hamza nodded.

'No.' Her voice was resolutely steady. Calm. Unsettling. She looked up.

'Nefyn?' Joseph hissed.

'*Un fi yw e,*' she replied. Joseph studied her face in disbelief. 'He stays here,' she said. Joseph shook his head. 'And you will sleep in the boathouse.' Nefyn's voice was studiously even.

'I . . . I can go and sleep there,' interjected Hamza.

'No,' Nefyn said, her eyes fixed on her brother.

'I'm trying to look after you,' Joseph said through his teeth. Nefyn laughed, a sudden lightness in her face. 'He'll be gone by this afternoon and you can forget about him.' Joseph's tone was softer now, wheedling.

'No.'

'Nefyn.'

'I said no!' There was a quiet fury in her now. 'You know what I'll do, Joseph.'

Joseph felt the weight of her words for a moment.

'*Paid â siarad felna . . .*' he replied.

'*Bydd ddistaw! Ti'n gwbod beth alla'i neud,*' she threatened.

Hamza watched as Joseph was cowed. An unintelligible exchange. A sudden vulnerability about him. Joseph was looking at her in fury. He turned. Spat on the floor. Grabbed his bag and left.

Nefyn sat on the bench, looking out to sea. Hamza came outside, sat beside her in silence. It was clearer this evening, the fog's opaqueness thinning, allowing for glimmers of the sea's opalescent blues.

He had stayed inside for hours, his guilt growing. Like water, he had trickled into their home and, having frozen there, inflexible, he had split them apart.

Sometimes, it took only a little to split boulders; a small insidious trickling into an infinitesimal vulnerability could split countries. Water or blood. Both could create this particular misery.

'I'm sorry,' he said eventually, 'I know you didn't ask for this.'

'Neither did you,' she replied, keeping her attention on the sea. It was restless this evening. Small white waves over its surface. Seabirds rising and falling with the wind.

'Will he tell anyone I'm here?'

Nefyn shook her head. Hamza thought for a moment of the look on Joseph's face when he left.

'What did you say to him? What language was that?'

'*Cymraeg*,' she whispered, suddenly sad, 'it's what my mother spoke. What we speak around here.'

'It sounded beautiful,' Hamza said quietly. Nefyn smiled, her eyes still on the sea.

'Some people think it's like speaking with ashes. But when I'm angry. The words . . . they catch light.' Hamza watched as the birds fought the breeze, remaining entirely still in the evening sky. 'Joseph and I were born together,' she said softly. 'We were so close. I always knew when he was in trouble; it was something else besides words. But he's . . . it's like he doesn't have a centre any more.' Nefyn looked cold, and instinctively Hamza placed his arm around her.

'Come,' he said.

She allowed herself to rest against him as he looked out at the startling beauty of the sea. His eyes were still becoming accustomed to its vastness, its restlessness, after the deadening stillness of his cell. They listened a while to the sea breathing.

'I had a compass once. When I didn't know where to turn, it was as if it gave me a place. A place to start from. Whatever lay ahead, I knew where I was somehow.'

Nefyn listened as his words were stolen by the breeze.

'What happened to it?' she asked.

'It was thrown into the sea,' he said quietly, 'just before I was.' He smiled. They sat in silence again.

'Do you think that I'm ill?' she asked. She didn't dare look into his face but her body stiffened under his arm as he considered.

'I've seen how people treat each other in this world.' He paused, gathering his thoughts. 'You received me without judgement. With kindness. With acceptance. I think that maybe you are well. It is everyone else on this Earth that is sick.'

17

Harbour ✦ *Harbwr* ✦ *Mina'*

Efa laid her arm across the bed and realized that he wasn't there. The sheets had been pushed back, the bed cold. She opened her eyes. He was gone. She descended the stairs calling his name, her panic rising with each step. The front door was open. Her heart sank. She pulled a coat off the bottom bannister and ran outside, the moon strong enough not to need a torch. The gate was open, too.

He had wandered off in the supermarket before, sometimes failed to find his way back from the gents in cafés, but he had never walked out of the house. Efa instinctively turned left down into the village, the way they usually took, because the pavement seemed to tip you that way down the slope. She shouted his name, but nothing came back except the barking of dogs and the sound of her own voice reverberating in the empty street.

She thought about what they had discussed before bed, combed her mind for any clues as she walked, her coat opening to reveal the white cotton nightdress underneath.

'Emrys!'

It was quiet. She scanned the road, up and down. Cursed herself for having slept so soundly. It was just that he had seemed so settled. The night before he had been crying in his sleep and calling out for his mother.

She had been unable to console him or convince him of who she was. Anything to make the calling stop, for her heart's sake as much as his. His clumsiness meant he was dirtying his clothes much more than usual; she had spent the day doing the laundry and, with it being so cold, everything took so long to dry.

'Emrys?'

The harbourside was quiet. Nothing but the gentle rocking of boats, their lines slapping on the masts occasionally and the moon setting a path across the water. 'Emrys?' Her voice sounded around the harbour walls.

'Yes?'

Efa stopped. Her breathing laboured.

'Where are you?'

He was standing by the slipway into the harbour. Alone. Feet from the water.

'We're taking the new boat out today,' he said. 'Have I forgotten something?'

Efa stopped. He was barefoot. His thin pyjamas hanging loose on his wasted shoulders.

'Emrys, what are you doing here?'

He laughed as she embraced him.

'Working. What do you think? What's wrong with you?' Efa felt her face crumple. Warm tears on his shoulder. 'What on earth's the matter?' He stroked the back of her head. Thirty years of rising at four in order to be at the harbour by five had ingrained themselves. And the repetitiveness had worn grooves in his memory and, occasionally, the pin of his mind would find them as his consciousness swirled and an old familiar routine would resurface. Crackle with static. Emrys felt his wife sob on his shoulder. 'I won't go today, then,' he said into her hair, an instinct to comfort her. 'Not if you don't want me to.'

They stood, as dawn began to stir, a leaving delayed, their arms wrapped tightly around each other.

❦

Joseph woke and squinted against the morning light. His mouth dry, the smell of vomit near by. He sat up, his arms and back aching from having slept on the hard floor. He tried to focus. He rubbed his face. She was still there, looming above him. His father's boat. He remembered looking at her, the night before, bottle of brandy in hand. He hadn't looked at her since she was dragged up the beach after his death. He'd thought of the way his father was tied to her as he breathed his last, Joseph unsure whether she had tried to save him or drown him. His father had bragged about the hours he and the shipwright had put into her. To perfect her. How he had smoothed his rough hands over her, elevated her to perfection. Joseph only ever saw her as a boat, a beautiful one, yes, but she didn't sing in his mind the way she did for his father. They had had to cut the ropes, cut his body from her in death – not that he could remember much about that day, except that he had lain awake during the storm, watching the waves thunder in. He had prayed, too. At sixteen years old, he'd stayed there until his back ached, his knees numb on the wooden floor, but his father had still died. Death, it seemed to Joseph, had come to him slowly. With the leaving of his wife, the reincarnation of her face in Nefyn's, and his separation from the boat.

He remembered looking at the boat last night, drawing the tarpaulin away before walking back towards the village. Towards The Ship. He had talked to some old acquaintances there, heard about the Doctor's funeral. The theories circulating. Talk of some plainclothed officers going door to door. Something was going on. Joseph kept quiet. Held on to his whiskey glass a little tighter. Feigned ignorance. After all, he had only just come home. The usual teasing over his 'fishing trip'. A distraction at least. Then there was a man, by the bar. Fair-haired. Big talk in his drink. Bitterness in his words. He said there was more to all this than they could ever imagine. Joseph had watched him down his drink and smirk as he walked away.

18

Gofyn ✦ *Enquiry* ✦ *Tahqiq*

THE MEN CAME TO the door early. Efa hadn't slept since coming home. She had lain Emrys down, talked to him gently until he had drifted off. He was still asleep now. They were doing a search, nothing to worry about. Wanted her to open the empty properties by the harbour for them. They showed their papers. She wanted to know if they had permission from the homeowners and they said they did. She couldn't leave Emrys upstairs alone, so reluctantly went next door to ask Mary if she would sit with him until lunchtime. Mary saw the policemen and acquiesced immediately, the temptation of a little drama too much to resist.

They started with the first property on the row that faced the harbour, and walked through each room methodically. Efa stood in the hallway of each house as they checked the doors and windows for signs of damage, the beds and kitchens for signs of use. Efa asked what they were looking for but they just smiled and said it was nothing to worry about. Efa could hear them opening attic hatches too, to shine torch-lights into the dark. Despite herself, she tried to draw them into a little small talk, see who they were looking for, but they weren't falling for it. It took most of the morning to check the ten houses, Efa standing around, looking out at the sea from each one as the men invaded every room. They thanked her politely, gave her a card with their contact details and asked her to report any-thing and anyone unusual. Efa watched them walk to their car.

Mary questioned her when she arrived home. Emrys still in his pyjamas, drinking tea at the table. She kissed his head lightly. She didn't know what they wanted, no. No, they didn't say where they were from. Maybe there were burglars around. You could never be too careful. Efa persuaded her out of the door as politely as she could, thanking her over and over for her help. She leant against it, closed her eyes. They had asked her whether she looked after any other proper-ties, and her mind had gone to Nefyn and the cottage. She shook her head. She had assumed that Joseph was back. Hoped he was. After all, she didn't like to think of her there alone, especially if the police were looking for someone.

Although Nefyn had tried to assure him that Joseph wouldn't betray him, Hamza had woken throughout the night, his breathing shallow. He had risen early, asked Nefyn for every map in the cottage. She had spent the morning unearthing them from the folds of books, and boxes and frames. Nefyn watched him now as he studied them in silence, his fingers finding an impalpable Braille on their surface. He read their sym-bols. Tried to tease their lines into showing him an exit. She watched as he charted the coast, sought out the tides. He knew that his best hope was the sea, every other avenue would be heavily guarded, but he'd need contacts, passage . . . He held his head in his hands. Felt Nefyn's eyes on him.

'What is it?' she asked.

He looked up at her. Frustration in his eyes. Looked once again at the maps.

'Nothing.'

'Don't lie,' she answered. Hamza had been pre-occupied all day. Quiet. The ease into which they had entered destabilized by his withdrawal. He looked up at her again. 'I'm going to need more help. If I can get to France, Germany perhaps. Maybe I can make my way . . .' He had been watching her. She too had been unable to settle anywhere today, had spent most of the day in her room, door closed. The argument with Joseph obviously weighing on her. He had considered her state of mind. Her ability to help him.

'Can you think of someone who could help? I'm willing to go myself. Meet someone, maybe at night . . .' he offered. He could tell that she was troubled. 'I'm sorry to ask.' She was looking away now.

'I'll try and think of someone,' she said softly. 'I promise.' Hamza nodded. Unwilling to push her further. They listened to the silence for a moment as Nefyn came to sit. She looked at the maps, reached out her fingertips.

'I've never really looked at them,' she said quietly. 'They've been here all these years.' She withdrew her fingers and looked up at him uncertainly. 'I hadn't noticed they were so beautiful.' Hamza watched her, dark circles under her eyes, her lids heavy.

'These are only one kind of map,' he said, 'the kind made by white men who put themselves at the centre of them.' He smiled. 'Muhammad ibn Musa al-Khwarizmi, Muhammad al-Idrisi . . . These men charted the world long ago . . . long before these maps here.'

There was a fondness in his eyes now, a familiar tenderness for the ancient mapmakers he had studied and taught. Hamza sat back in his seat. 'You know there are other peoples that sing their maps, link their songs to the stars to know where they are.' Hamza shrugged. 'A map is just a way of thinking about the world,' he said, 'but it can sometimes tell you more about the one making it than anything else.' Nefyn smiled. 'The military, they map places, use helicopters. Aerial photography, but the world doesn't work like that. Doesn't give away its secrets so easily.' There was a stillness in his face now as he continued. 'There are caves, overhanging rocks, places they cannot see if they only look from above. Things hidden in shadows.' Hamza shook his head. 'If you want to map a place properly, you must feel it. Know it. That is what they do not understand.'

Nefyn nodded, watched as he overlaid map after map, studying their contours, a growing agitation inside her. As the light weakened, she made her way outside. She could hear the water in the cove below. Deep and dark. The light of the moon weighing on the tide. The nightjars calling. The sight of Hamza studying the maps had unsettled her. His searching. The way he had held his head in his hands, not knowing where to turn. She waited, until she heard him push back his chair, extinguish the light. She waited until she was sure that he was fast asleep before she got up, and made her way down to the cove.

19

Longitude • Khatu altuwl • Hydredd

Hamza woke early after a forced, fitful sleep. He got up stiffly, made his way to the kitchen. The door to Nefyn's room was ajar and he looked in on her instinctively but she wasn't there, her bed seemingly unslept-in. The morning light on the sheets. He listened for her but there was nothing save the sound of the gulls over the cottage. She must have made her way to the cove early. He walked into her room a few steps. It was simple, austere. Whitewashed walls, a deep-set window, an old wardrobe, the door open. He reached out to touch her clothes, all moss greens and blues. A single bed, a desk, rows of old books. There was a sense of simplicity here, and calm. Then, he caught sight of himself in a small mirror on her desk. His presence there suddenly obtrusive, obscene. He turned, feeling her absence grow.

The sun was weak today, watery. He brewed some coffee, the cup clattering in the silence. He sat watching it steam, tasted its bitterness. Longed for the sweet coffee that he and his friends would drink at his brother's house, its cardamom aftertaste. His sister-in-law's laughter. Their warmth. The way Hussein would run to her and the way she would throw him up into the air. Head back. Laughing. Over the years, he had consoled himself with visions of Hussein tucked under his sister-in-law's arm, reading, his uncle promising him that his father would be found. Other times, he had tortured himself, convincing himself that he would have been told the worst in order to spare him hope. Hamza got up. Listened to the sea a moment.

The lack of Nefyn changed the cottage elementally. Its sounds and colours. The walls seemed more oppressive somehow, the stone greyer. His mind returned to what he had asked of her, her promise to find someone to help him, apprehension building in him as he thought of her silence. The way she withdrew. He thought he heard the sound of the door, but it was only the seaweed that hung there to forecast the weather, scratching the door in the breeze. He considered following her down to the cove, but the risk of being seen or encountering Joseph worried him. He would have to trust that she would come back.

He tipped the coffee grounds into the sink and turned, pulling one of Joseph's old jumpers over his head as he went. The clothes smelled of oil and salt and wool, and even though they were not his, he was grateful for them, their character an antidote to the anonymity of the ones given to him in jail. He moved through the living room, and opened the door. His impotency had gnawed at him in his restless sleep, and he had listened to the breeze in the roof as he lay. At least it would be something for him to do until Nefyn came home.

The tiles were scattered around the cottage. Some broken, others unharmed except for having been ripped asunder by the force of the storm. He gathered them up carefully, stacked them by the back door. He found a small lean-to shed of zinc filled with tools, black and oily. And a ladder, rope, nails. He stuffed some of the latter into his pockets. Picked up a hammer and dragged out the ladder. He made his way to the front of the cottage and leant it on the eaves. It wasn't a high building, but the breeze was mischievous this morning, plucking at the ladder wilfully. He pushed the hammer into the waistband of his trousers before hauling some slates up under his arm. He would start on one side, and work his way towards the other until the roof was once more secure.

He felt his body warm with the movement, the dull ache in his ribs making itself known again. The sky was heavy with rain and the gulls wheeled noisily overhead as he hammered. He tried to match the tiles, push them under the ones above so as to make the seal watertight. There was already a hole in each one, made by a more skilled hand decades ago, so all he had to do was position them, nail them home.

There would be storms at home, too – snowstorms, and the occasional storms of sand when the desert would be flung into the air. There would be nothing to do except stay inside, watch as the world turned sepia, the sun disappearing. They would last for hours, sometimes days, and the fine red dust would leave a film on any surface – cars, windows, the insides of your lungs. His father used to say that it was a good reminder that they came from dust and would return to it. His mother would scold him, saying that he did not have to keep the house and their clothes clean so it was easy for him to say. When he was a boy, Hamza would struggle to breathe as the world disappeared. As he got older, the fighting, the dust clouds and sandstorms seemed to intermingle, making the outside world appear as if it were crumbling, dissipating in front of his eyes. The wind caught his breath; it was still cold. Sharp. Burning his face. He hammered another tile in place before descending the ladder, moving it and climbing up once more.

He tried not to look across towards the cliff edges as he worked, tried not to look for her. She would be back soon; the sun was overhead by now. He continued with the work, stopping only to descend the ladder and gather more tiles. He had just nailed the last one in place when he heard footsteps. His heart gladdened as he turned, his back towards the eaves of the cottage, one foot on the top rung of the ladder when he heard the voice.

'I need more clothes.'

It was Joseph. Pale in the spring light. He was smaller than Hamza remembered. 'Where is she?'

He climbed slowly down the ladder.

'She's not here.' Hamza suddenly became aware of his own breathing. Joseph measured him with his eyes. Walked forward a little.

'They're looking for you ... you know that?' Hamza could smell his breath was sour. 'It's only a matter of time till they find you.' Hamza didn't answer. Joseph looked away. 'You know she's not right,' he said, 'you know that.' Hamza resisted the temptation to retaliate. 'She's ill and you're taking advantage of it. You're making her worse because you need her,' Joseph said, studying Hamza's face.

'No,' Hamza replied, the voice coming from deep inside. Nefyn's absence was pressing on him. He wanted Joseph to know that he was wrong, but the fact that she still hadn't returned was weighing on his tongue, making it heavy. 'She's not ill,' he said at last.

Joseph let out a bitter laugh.

'You have no idea what you're dealing with,' he said.

'Maybe not, but I know cruelty when I see it.'

Joseph's smile straightened.

'You don't know what you're talking about. You'll see.'

'I'll see what?'

'Where is she, then?' Joseph asked again, recognizing a certain wavering in Hamza's voice. The uncertainty in his face. 'Come on,' he pressed, moving closer so that he was inches from him, his breath on his face. He bore down on him in intimidation. 'Come on, tell me where she is.'

Hamza shook his head. 'I don't know.'

Joseph found himself smirking. 'Of course you don't,' he spat. Then, satisfied, he moved away and disappeared into the cottage.

Outside, Hamza waited. Listened as Joseph moved around inside the cottage, his very presence strangely violating. He saw him emerge, a bag on his back. He didn't even look in Hamza's direction.

'Tell her I'm staying in the village,' he said. Hamza watched him go, the mobile phone he had stolen from Joseph's pocket now in his.

20

Needle ◆ Nodwydd ◆ 'iibra

EFA WAS ON HER way to the post office when she saw his figure from afar. She recognized it instantly – the reddish hair, the strong shoulders. There were a few places offering beds for the evening that stayed open at this time of year. For walkers. Tradesmen. People like that. Efa watched as Joseph entered the narrow house by the harbour and her thoughts immediately turned to Nefyn. She had thought that she would be satisfied after seeing her, but instead her curiosity had grown. Efa's eyes would settle on a particular colour and she would be reminded of Nefyn's hair. The coolness of the morning light would bring her eyes to mind. She had thought of going straight home after paying her bills but she decided to go to the shop, so she would have an excuse, at least, to call by the cottage whilst Mary was sitting with Emrys. She wouldn't be long, after all.

Efa noticed the tightening in her stomach she always seemed to feel upon seeing the small windswept cottage. She pulled up, took a box from the back seat and carried it to the door. It was getting dark and the waves were echoing noisily below in the cove. She noticed that the tiles had been replaced on the roof, that the door of the lean-to was closed. She left the box of food on the bench as usual, before walking towards the door, fighting the urge to look in through the windows. She knocked and waited. Studied her cold knuckles. The way the skin was dry there, her hands being in and out of water all the time. She knocked again. No answer. Efa's disappointment was physical. Perhaps her previous encounter had encouraged her too much. Grown in her mind. She felt her cheeks flush despite the cold. The small warmth she had thought she had felt from Nefyn; she had thought that she could somehow cultivate it. She turned, scolding herself as she walked, her mood darkening. Because she could not help herself, she turned one last time to look at the cottage and she was sure she caught sight of a figure. A man. Standing in the window, looking out.

Hamza had stared at the phone for a moment, his hands trembling. The first and second numbers he had remembered brought nothing but continuous dial tones. His brother's phone, his parents. He cut off the calls, his mind racing, breathlessly repeating sequences of numbers he thought he knew. Trying not to drop the phone. The third number, a mobile number for Khalid, one of the few colleagues he could trust, had been answered. He'd listened. It was a young man's voice. Khalid's nephew. He'd tried to explain. He'd asked him about Hussein. But there was nothing but confusion. He didn't know anything. He begged him not to hang up. He'd promised to contact his uncle. Then, the phone's battery died.

Hamza looked at it. The dead greyness of the screen. Its unyielding buttons. Then, he screamed, threw it across the room. Paced. His stomach hurting. Wondering whether he'd squandered his chance, his opportunity. It was only then that he heard the sound of a car door closing outside, dropping to the floor so as not to be seen. He tried to control his breathing as he heard someone knock at the door. Footsteps moving about. He saw a weak shadow on the floor, a looming presence at the window. His throat constricting as he pressed himself to the cold stones. The walls were so thick that he had not been able to judge whether the person had gone. He had no sense of time or direction. When he got up, he saw the figure of a woman. Her head just turning away. He pressed himself to the wall again but he was sure she had seen him. She must have seen him.

Afterwards, he had paced once more, picking up the phone to check it in vain. He considered leaving immediately. He could hike across the country, hide here and there, but he knew his chances of success would be pitiful. He could not believe how foolish he'd been. To have been seen. So simply. So unnecessarily. He knew that they could be on their way already. Perhaps Nefyn herself had gone to get help. His uncertainty grew with every minute that Nefyn was gone. His hearing sharpened so that he heard approaching footsteps every hour. He was sure he heard a helicopter, too. His mind wheeling back to Homs. The thundering air, bringing with it death and destruction. Everything that he had rebuilt, every small step of reparation, started to crumble in his mind. He saw faces in the stone walls. A sense of darkness encroaching, and when it did and there was still no sign of Nefyn, he had watched as the fire fell in on itself, and the gloom grew around him.

By the time Hamza had fallen asleep on the floor, the sky was black over the cottage, the stars lucid and sharp. Exhausted and spent, he did not hear Nefyn walk barefoot up from the cove and push the door open. He did not sense her feet leaving footprints on the slate floor, her clothes soaked through with sea-water. Her dark eyes sullen. He did not see her stand over him, watching him sleep, a compass hanging from a chain in her cold hand.

Dwfn • Deep • Eamiq

'NEFYN? NEFYN, WAKE UP!'
She was barely breathing.

'Nefyn?'

Her clothes were wet, dark. Sodden.

'Nefyn, please, where did you get this, Nefyn?'

Her eyes were dull. Her body was stiff. Her limbs leaden. She was lying on her bed, her hair clinging together with salt. The bedclothes were stained with dampness. He turned her on to her side. His hands trembling, the familiar weight of the compass in his hand. Her eyes rolled back in her head.

'*Al'ama*,' he swore.

He picked her up, an arm underneath her neck, the other under the crook of her knees. Carried her to the chair by the fire. Pulled the heavy wool cardigan from her shoulders, her arms. Her head was tilting to the side. He tugged her dress over her head. Rubbed her hands in his. He ran back to Joseph's room, yanked off the blanket, dropped it on the hearth. He pushed some twigs into the fireplace, tried to steady his hands long enough to strike a match. Then, he took off his own jumper. Dragged Nefyn to her feet. Wrapped his body around her, the blanket around his shoulders, and pressed her to him. She was frigid with cold. Icy. He tucked her head under his chin like a child, started praying through instinct. He pulled her down, towards the fire, all the time willing it to burn, to find its heat. He listened as it crackled, the fire finding its voice, creeping, catching. He could hear her heart beating against his. Slowly. She smelled of the sea. The movement of his chest rustling the compass on its chain. He opened his palm in disbelief and looked at the dial. Pressed it to his face, his lips, felt its familiar form on his skin. He clicked it open. There was no doubt about it – it was his, the pin spinning, unable to settle. He closed it once again, his stomach lurching as she started shivering in his arms. Her whole body convulsing. He held her, steadied her against him. It was still dark outside, the blackness dense and starless. She must have been searching for it. She must . . . He could not think of it. It didn't make sense. He felt the tremor in her body.

He had seen this kind of shivering before. A body in shock. When Fatima had given birth to Hussein. He had come into the world too quickly. Her body hadn't had time to adjust. As his slippery form was placed on her breasts, she convulsed. Both of them quivered, with the suddenness, the brutality of birth, the relentlessness of living things.

He held Nefyn for hours, feeling his own heat seep into her, leaving him cold and stiff. The shivering eventually stopped, as her body became accustomed to the idea of life again. Her breathing steadied. It was getting lighter now, the blue light of dawn somehow bluer against the whitewashed walls.

Hamza knew she was awake, without looking. Without asking.

'I saw him.' Hamza said the words slowly, as if

reasserting his own truth. 'I saw him throw the compass into the sea. I saw it with my own eyes.'

Nefyn was staring into the fire, the crown of her head under Hamza's chin.

'I wanted you to have it back,' she said, her voice clouding in the cold.

'Nefyn, this doesn't make sense. You could have killed yourself.'

Nefyn remained silent.

Hamza looked into her face. Pressed his thumbs on the dark circles under her eyes. Her skin deathly white.

'How? How did you do it?' Hamza searched her expression. His eyes pained. 'It's impossible,' he said again.

Nefyn shook her head. Heavy tears in her eyes.

'No, it's not.'

'But why?'

Hamza watched her as she cried, saw the sorrow in her face. The sorrow of hope, the heaviest burden anyone could carry. He had seen it in parents' faces watching over their injured children, and in the faces of the elderly nearing death. He held her once more, pressed her to him and kissed her head. The compass, still spinning, unable to settle between them in its case.

Joseph would have to find his own food in the evening. The landlady had made this clear. He'd given up looking for his phone, closed the door of the cramped room, walked down the carpeted stairs and turned up his collar against the wind before heading to The Ship. It was quiet apart from a group of men drinking by the bar. He ate in silence by the fire before ordering himself a beer. Their laughter seemed infectious and after a while one of them invited him to join them for a cigarette. Some of them worked on security at the base. They were talking about beer being so much cheaper at the barracks bar, but they just needed to get away sometimes. One or two of them he half recognized from around the place, and then there was the fair-haired man he had seen in The Ship before. Joseph was drinking hard tonight, the talk turning from women to money to football. They started drinking spirits, teasing the girl behind the bar enough for her eventually to call in some help. Two men arrived, told them to keep it down, to behave themselves, to leave. The fair-haired man squared up to one of them and Joseph felt something in the room change. He couldn't remember who threw the first punch, but he remembered the feeling of freedom. Of lashing out. The commotion. The getting thrown out, loud and swearing, on to the harbourside, where most of the younger men staggered home. Joseph shared a cigarette and laughter with the fair-haired man on the harbour wall. They laughed because Joseph's collar was torn, and the fair-haired man's lip was bleeding. They exhaled blue smoke into the dead night, the string of lights around the harbour blurry. The man confided that he had something better to smoke. So they smoked that, too. Relaxed. They were friends now. And he could tell Joseph a secret. Because they were brothers. He was a soldier at the barracks, and he'd almost been sacked because of a filthy fucking terrorist. The adrenaline was still warming both their bodies and the high of unleashing was still strong in their minds. He was out there. He knew it. They were looking for him on the quiet but it would only be fair if he found him first. Get some justice at least. Because he'd kill him, he said, if he found him. He'd fucking kill him.

22

East • Dwyrain • Alsharq

EMRYS HAD BEEN UNSETTLED today. Pacing. Caged in the house. He had taken all his old books down from the shelves and put them back in a different order. He'd done it over and over, unwilling to stop to eat or drink, as if he were arranging and rearranging the stories in his mind. He had shouted at her, too. Raised his arm sharply when she touched him so she had just retreated, sat and watched. Waited for him to exhaust himself. After that, he had sat by the window overlooking the sea, his mind preoccupied by the passing clouds, the shape of the coast, asking her over and over what he was seeing, the relationships between objects and their names loosening, the references of colour and form slipping away. He was asleep now in his chair and Efa had decided to leave him there.

She had asked a man to come and put some new locks on the outside door and she had started keeping the keys in her pocket at all times, but still she couldn't sleep. Every time she'd close her eyes, she'd see a dark figure framed in a whitewashed window. It was a man, she was sure of it, and they were looking for someone. The police. They must be looking for someone, and it wasn't Joseph.

Efa kicked back the covers; there was no point trying any more. She walked softly downstairs to make herself some tea. If she had noticed, how long would it be before someone else did? She waited for the kettle to boil, measured herself a spoonful of strong loose leaves. Nefyn and Joseph didn't keep company and Joseph's friends were mainly acquaintances on the boats, from what she could gather. They had no family left. She took her mug to her favourite chair at the window, overlooking the harbour in the distance, her thoughts running backwards like the tide receding. Back to Nefyn's mother, Arianell.

Arianell had refused to be baptized, but still wanted to take Holy Communion. The vicar had not allowed it, saying she would have to be cleansed with holy water first. She had wanted to receive His body and His blood, but could not bring herself to see herself as dirty. To admit sin. Efa had taken her side, tried to talk to the congregation, but they had turned their backs. The place where Nefyn's mother came to find peace became a place of judgement. She would still see her there, though. The church remained unlocked and Efa would clean it regularly as per the rota. She would sometimes find Arianell weeping quietly in the back pew. She tolerated Efa, not because she showed her compassion perhaps, but because she allowed her to feel her rage without trying to sympathize or cajole. Efa had seen the bruises on her body, the rolled-down sleeve of her blouse. Everyone knew about Nefyn's father.

To this day, she didn't know quite why she'd done it. Efa held the keys to the sacristy, where the cleaning cupboards were. She had pushed the key into the lock. Opened the chest where the wafers of bread and wine were kept and carried them to her. Arianell had watched

Efa coming down the aisle, watched her sit in the pew at the front. Place the sacramental cup down before bowing her head and praying, her back to the altar. Their whispers combined and echoed around them as they finished. Then, Efa placed some bread on to her palm. Watched as she pressed her lips to it and crossed herself. Efa then held the cup to her mouth. The jewelled colour of the lights through the window illuminating them both. She watched as she drank. Her tired face, her thirst. Her hand over Efa's hand as she swallowed. She closed her eyes and Efa saw the tears slide silently down her face. And there they sat, in that cold church, a communion of women. That was the last time she saw her. A few weeks later she had gone. Disappeared. He said that she had left him but Efa was never so sure. He had a boat. She was terrified. Weaker than him. Efa had vowed to herself then that she would try to look after Nefyn as much as she would allow. When news came of her father's death, Efa did not grieve, felt only relief mixed with a concern about the children. They were both so young.

She looked out, the light lingering longer as spring started making its presence felt. She would have to go and see Nefyn. She wouldn't rest until she had.

⁓

Hamza had watched her as the light grew around them. They had lain intertwined, their bodies borderless. Each reviving the other, sharing their warmth. They had not kissed, but had simply lain, her back to his chest, listening to each other breathing. The strange closeness of someone else. After she fell asleep, her head heavy on his arm, Hamza had held her against him. The thin skin of her freckled shoulder under his chin.

He looked at the compass in the half-light. It wasn't impossible that she had found it. It might have been brought to shore just like he had. But it was heavy – surely it would have sunk, been dragged to the depths and lain there, immovable. She must have swum. Swum into the sea and looked for it. But the expanse? The size of the compass? He had tried to find out, but she had given no more explanation and the shadows under her eyes made him reluctant to ask again.

She was warmer now, her hair still thick with salt. The act of kindness that almost killed her. Hamza had considered himself blessed. His mother had believed that kindness was a child's best teacher. That scolding would only work temporarily. Fatima was the same with Hussein. She would see things through his eyes, kneel close to him. A certain softness in her that she reserved for him only. And when she was tired, overcome, she would place him in Hamza's arms, go for a walk. She believed that shouting at a child was beneath her, that it was the same as becoming a child again yourself. Her quiet, instinctive understanding of Hussein's needs – he recognized it in Nefyn, something achingly familiar.

His mind returned to the crackly voice on the other end of the phone. The first time he had heard his language for years. Its cadences, its rhythms. The fact that his colleague might somehow know by now that he was alive. A growing resolve inside him as the glimpse of home made him hunger for more. He watched as she started to stir. Her green eyes staring before looking around, disorientated. She stayed a moment in his arms, in complete stillness, before pulling herself away from him and going to her room, looking back at him as she closed the door. He lay and listened as she washed and dressed.

They ate breakfast in silence, the compass rotating between them on the table. *Tramontana. Greco. Levante. Scirocco. Osto. Libeccio. Ponente. Maestro.* Both watching as the pin turned, restlessly, from one direction to another and another. He looked up.

'Nefyn?' He waited for her to look at him. 'When you were gone, your brother came, I . . . I took his phone . . .'

Nefyn's gaze didn't waver. Her face pale.

'I called home.'

Nefyn smiled, her eyes unreadable.

'I hope, I think, that maybe my friend knows I'm alive . . . But then someone called here, I was seen. I'll have to leave,' he said.

Her face became troubled.

'Who saw you?' Her voice was even.

'An old woman came. I'm sure she saw me.'

'What did she look like?'

'She was older, skirt, a scarf around her neck . . . heavy coat.'

Nefyn nodded as he described Efa.

'You don't need to worry about her. She won't have told anyone.'

'How do you know?'

'I know . . .' Nefyn thought for a moment. 'Efa, she brings me food when Joseph is away. He always told me that she couldn't be trusted but she can.'

Hamza took this in.

'I wish I'd never listened to him. Those tablets he gave me. I couldn't think.'

'Your brother said they're looking for me.'

Nefyn studied him, her strength returning to her body. Her senses. He was scared, Nefyn could see that. His breath had become short, his chest tightening. Her eyes dropped to the spinning compass once more.

'I've been thinking about your father's boat,' he said. 'The one in the boathouse.'

Nefyn followed his train of thought. 'Can you sail?'

'Yes, but not well.'

'We should go and look at it tomorrow.'

Hamza nodded. He did not know how feasible the plan was, but it seemed like his only choice.

'Perhaps your friend Efa can help us,' he offered gently.

Nefyn's face softened, her eyes warming at Efa's name.

'Yes, I'm sure she'll help us.'

Hamza nodded but she wasn't looking at him now, she was studying the compass whose pin had been slowing as they talked. It trembled on its axis, and eventually stopped. Nefyn looked up. *Levante*.

23

Dŵr • Water • Ma'

JOSEPH WOKE IN THE guest house, sweating and thirsty. He lay there, eyes wide open, before running to the bathroom to vomit. Back in his room, clothes strewn on the floor, flickers of the night before revisited him; the stiffness of his limbs, the pounding of his head – the whiskey. He looked across at the glass of water on the table but couldn't muster the strength to reach out for it. He had paid the woman for a week, almost all the money he had left. Soon he would have to leave, return to the boats in the North. He listened to the sea, the poorly glazed windows allowing a draught to pull at the flowery curtains.

He was cut adrift. He knew that. The way Nefyn looked at that man. All those years he'd taken care of her – forgotten. He'd never thought it would be this way. He had known that this time might come, but assumed he would be the one to force the change. And he had wished for it. Over and over. To not be defined by her. But now that he was free, he couldn't move. He thought for a moment of a storm petrel he had caught as a child. Its broken wing, the way he looked after it. And when, in triumph, he stood on the cliff and threw it into the air on its recovery, it fluttered down to his feet. He threw it again, longing to see it soar, but it wouldn't leave. He ignored it, for days, until he found its lifeless body on the cliffs one morning. Perhaps it had tried to show him how futile it was to intervene in fate. Perhaps he should have learnt from it.

Head pounding, he pulled himself up, undid the buttons on his shirt and realized that his collar had ripped. He frowned. His hand was shaking. He remembered being at The Ship. Eating. Drinking. He had seen the other fathers take their sons to The Ship when they came of age. Buy them a drink. He'd had to navigate it by himself. A more ramshackle introduction: bottles of whiskey on boats, vomiting whilst old seamen looked on and laughed. He'd had to learn quickly. The way they made him feel like a man and then simultaneously treated him like a boy.

He reached for the water, drank deeply and then regretted it as the cold liquid lay heavy in his stomach. He was accustomed to sleeping for shifts of three or four hours through the night on the boats, could sleep through the hardest of gales. Get up, shock himself into work, get shouted at, soaked by the cold spray. The churning of engines and the tension of ropes threatening to overwhelm him. You had to keep on your toes. All it took was a loop of rope around your ankle, the sway of the boat, and you'd be in and gone. An arm in a chain pulley. As he grew, he began to find his place, squaring up to one or two of them as his shoulders filled out, and they left him alone. In this way, he could live. Hauling, and pulling fish from the sea, his knife ready to gut, packing fish in ice, their stunned eyes staring.

And now he remembered it, the argument. Someone he didn't know. He felt suddenly breathless, hungry for air. He swung his legs over the side of the bed, leant forward. Something. Someone had said *something*. He got up, his legs stiff and unsteady, and walked to the window. Pushed the curtains back, pulled the greying nets to one side. He tried to unlock the sash windows, to pull them up, but they were glued shut with old paint. He leant against the cool glass and looked out at the harbour, the tension in his chest worsening. It was quiet this morning, and still. He saw the dull grey sea and the harbour wall and then he remembered. The fair-haired man. Their laughter. The things that he had said, and what Joseph had said in return. His eyes widened, a sudden weakness spreading through his body.

Both Nefyn and Hamza knew that they must go to the boat but neither of them was in a hurry. Their separation would soon come and would already be painful enough. They dressed, the doors to each room open, and Nefyn tied back her hair. Hamza pulled the chain of the compass over his head.

This morning, the air was more blue than grey. A light breeze blew the grasses on the cliffs. The sea, touched with a sullen jade green. They made their way down the path, the wind pulling at their clothes. Nefyn reached the cove first, her familiar route to the strandline now untrodden. She kept watch whilst Hamza moved towards the boatshed, pulled open the door. The air was musty, dark. Joseph's empty bottles on the floor, the smell of urine, dust lit up in the cold air. He pulled at the tarpaulin, squinted. Pushed open the door further to get more light. He wished he had paid more attention to his grandfather. His skills. He walked the length of her, looking for damage. Knelt down, lay on his back to squeeze under the hull, his hands feeling for any roughness on her bows. Some loose timber. He got up again. Looked around. There were tools here, some parts. As the list of things they would require grew in his mind, the difficulty of it all made him throw down the tarpaulin once again.

He heard a familiar voice behind him. He stood stock-still, his hearing sharpening. The sound of foot-steps on the shale. He stepped away, behind the door. A figure approaching. He saw Nefyn turn towards it. Hamza recognized him immediately. The way he walked. He was shouting, shouting at Nefyn. Drunk? It was difficult to tell. Hamza knew who he was look-ing for. He felt his body suddenly pulled tight. He watched as he approached her, his gait wild, unsteady. Some words exchanged. Nefyn held her ground, but his movements suggested an agitation that Hamza wasn't prepared to risk. He knew Nefyn wouldn't betray his presence, that it would be up to him. He watched as he got closer to her. The anger, the kindling inside him growing, snapping, taking hold.

'I'm here!' Hamza shouted. His whole body suddenly full of adrenaline. He walked out of the darkness, felt the light of day on his face. He was tired of hiding. The figure spun around.

'It's me you want.' Hamza stood there in the open, his arms by his sides. Owens turned towards him. Laughed loudly, bitterly. Hamza started walking towards him.

'Well, well, well ... here he is ... the invisible man ...' said Owens, savouring every moment. Hamza noticed that he was unsteady on his feet. Nefyn's eyes flicked to Hamza's face. She saw that he knew him. 'They're looking for you all over.' His voice was brimming with contempt. As Hamza neared him, he signalled Nefyn to move backwards to safety, but she stood still. Owens stuck out his chin, his words running into each other. 'You think you're clever, don't you? Eh?'

'No.'

'Scum like you should be stamped out.'

Nefyn's eyes fell to the man's waistband. The handle of a knife, just above his belt loop. She looked up again at Hamza. Shook her head imperceptibly in warning.

'You'd happily see us all dead, wouldn't you?' Owens said. Hamza could smell alcohol on his breath. 'Just because we don't live like you. Think like you.'

Owens leant nearer, his words making him look older somehow. Nefyn could see the despair on Hamza's face.

'What do you want?' asked Hamza.

Owens flicked his head upwards.

'I want you to come with me. And we're going to march right back to the barracks, into that fucking Lieutenant Colonel's office, and we're going to blow their whole story wide open.'

Nefyn listened to the sea, the way it churned the stones as it turned them in the tide. Knocked off the hard edges.

'I can't do that.'

Owens smiled.

'I don't think you understand. You're still a prisoner. I'm still the guard here. I'm not asking you, I'm telling you.' Then he turned his gaze to Nefyn.

'No,' Hamza repeated.

Owens turned his head sharply. Laughed. Drew the knife from his waistband, and held it in front of him.

'Or we could do this another way.'

'Don't do this,' said Nefyn.

Owens smirked. 'You don't know him.'

Hamza and Owens stared at each other. Eye to eye. He moved closer, his breath on Hamza's face. 'Thought you'd got away, didn't you?' Hamza noticed the sweat on his face, his brow. 'Now, come with me,' he said again, pressing the blade of his knife nearer to Hamza. Hamza felt his anger consolidate into something harder. His jaw clenched in fury.

'No,' he said, pushing the words out, 'I will not.'

Hamza braced as Owens raised his hand to lunge at him. Nefyn closed her eyes. Hamza flinched, and waited for the strike of the knife, but then Owens's face changed. He stopped. His arm mid-air. He looked up at his hand, and watched as the knife dropped to the floor, clattered on the stones beneath their feet, its blade blunting. Nefyn opened her eyes and the guard turned to look at her. Slowly. Deliberately. Their eyes locked. She smiled at him. Comfortingly. And then Hamza watched as he turned again, turned away and started walking. As though his mind was broken. He walked towards the sea. Hamza watched as Nefyn's dispassionate eyes followed him. Over the strandline.

His arms by his sides. He didn't flinch at all at the cold. He seemed completely and utterly calm as he kept walking, walking into the sea.

⁓

Joseph ran back from the cove, along the coast towards the village, his heart pounding, his feet failing to find a foothold sometimes along the rocky path. The village came into view, he stopped and retched, but there was nothing in his stomach. He spat, trying to clear the strangling sensation from his throat. He straightened up, the wind catching his hair.

He had seen the man walk into the water. His thighs pressing on until he had disappeared, leaving only a ripple on the sea's smooth surface. He had wanted to shout but his voice became stuck in his throat. He gasped for air on the headland. Looked out to sea. Down at the village. His breath was settling again. The cold wind cooling the sweat on his back.

She knew he had seen her. He knew she did. For when the man had walked into the sea, she had looked upwards towards the cliff to exactly where he was standing and he was sure that he had seen a soft smile on her face.

24

Cyfaill • Friend • Sadiq

HAMZA KEPT PACING THE floor. Running his fingers through his hair. His eyes darting everywhere.

'I don't understand, Nefyn.'

She was standing. Passive. Hands by her sides.

'What happened? What happened there?'

She shrugged. Hamza stopped walking, came towards her, held her hands in his. His eyes searching her face.

'Did you do that? Did you make him do it?'

She looked away.

'Nefyn!'

She could feel his heart thundering in his chest.

'I didn't touch him,' she said softly.

He let her hands go.

'I know you didn't *touch* him, I saw.'

He stepped backwards again, his hands on his sides.

He looked at her. Her face framed by her dark hair. Her thin limbs. Fragile. Steely. 'What else? What else can you do?' He brought his hands to his face. Laughed. Incredulously. 'What else are you capable of, Nefyn?'

Nefyn looked up at him.

'We are all capable of anything.'

He stood, his fingers over his mouth. His smile fading.

'What does that mean?'

Nefyn tilted her head.

'Nefyn, what does that mean?'

Nefyn stood silent a moment. 'I never asked you what you did or didn't do . . . *why* you were a prisoner. What you were capable of. I trusted you.'

Hamza felt her words settle on him heavily. He exhaled.

'I've been so blind. What are you involved with?' he said.

'You asked me once if I would trust you, and I did. That's all I want in return.'

There was no judgement in her eyes, only a challenge, her gaze hardening.

The knock on the door startled them both. Hamza's eyes darted to Nefyn's face. He held his breath.

'It's Efa,' said Nefyn softly, 'the old woman.'

His breathing when he exhaled was still laboured. She looked up at him.

'Do you trust me?'

Hamza searched her face. He thought about what he had seen. What she had told him. Found himself nodding. Nefyn walked to the door. Looked back at him once more before opening it. Hamza watched as she let Efa in. There was a moment's hesitation before Efa came into view. She looked at Nefyn and then at him, her face suddenly ashen.

'I knew you had someone here,' she said.

'Efa, I've never asked anything of you, but I need your help now. I'm asking for it.'

Efa looked at them both.

'He's a friend and I need to look after him.'

Efa's hands were knotted together, her shoulders tense. She sensed something different about Nefyn. It was as if she had somehow grown.

'Of course,' she nodded and looked at Hamza, 'of course.'

Nefyn had been quiet since Efa left. Had refused to look at him. Hamza had cooked some rice, tried to keep his hands, his mind occupied, had brought it to her by the fire, but she had left it untouched, got up, and walked barefoot outside.

The sight of the guard walking into the water played over and over in Hamza's mind. His fixed stare, the way his shoulders had dropped. Then, as the darkness spilled into the cottage, he followed her outside, found her sitting on the cliff-top amongst the silver grasses, her legs over the edge. He watched her for a moment before moving to sit beside her, his heels dislodging pebbles from the crumbling cliff face under his feet. They both listened as the stones fell away into the darkness below.

Hamza sat looking out at the rippling water, willing the words to come to him. The night was calm, the stars heavy, low in the sky and glistening. Hamza took in their stillness. Their literal truth.

'The first maps were maps of stars,' he said quietly, the breeze catching his hair, his shirt. Nefyn did not stir.

'When they were bombing my city, they would bomb any light. Bomb any lamp, any flame, any sign of life. They plunged the city into darkness. But then came the stars.' Hamza looked across at her. 'They had always been there. Hidden. And when the darkness came to the city, it was like the stars were mocking the bombers . . . letting them know how small they were. It became easier to sleep then; I wasn't so afraid of closing my eyes when the stars were like that. It was as if they were reminding us that there is something more to this world beyond what we understand.'

Nefyn listened.

'He would have killed you, you know that,' she murmured, her face unmoving.

'I know,' he answered eventually.

'It wasn't a choice you or I made.'

The tide was thinning, receding, unveiling the gaping dark seabed below. Hamza stared at the thin line of water.

'How long have you . . .' he sought out the words, 'how long have you been like this?' Nefyn's face hardened, afraid to look at him for what she might see in his eyes.

'I told you the truth . . .'

'And your brother?'

Nefyn shook her head. 'He's not like me.'

'You have gifts?'

Nefyn thought for a moment.

'Joseph doesn't see it like that.'

Hamza shook his head.

'You can't live like this . . . You can't let your brother . . . Nefyn . . . look at me . . .'

Nefyn turned her eyes, looked at him, her expression darkening.

'I watched what this world did to my mother, and it will happen to me,' she said.

Hamza shook his head.

'That is not your future. Is this enough, Nefyn? How many years have you been hiding?'

She was looking at him now.

'It's not enough for me, and I doubt if it is enough for you.'

Nefyn's eyes were drawn back to the water. They listened to the far-away sea. 'I don't even know if there's anyone left,' she said. Hamza smiled, took her hand, pressed his thumb to her palm. Mapped the veins of her inner wrist, blue under her transparent skin like underground rivers.

'You know, when we got married, I gave Fatima a globe, a globe of the stars. They used to think that each star had its own sphere, that each one circled the Earth untouched and untouching.'

Nefyn watched as he circled her wrist with his fingers.

'But stars, they collide, they move, are never fixed . . . Making them appear so makes us feel better, but they stray into each others' paths, feel the pull of others, and that is the wonder of it.'

Nefyn felt the warmth of him on her right shoulder. His closeness. A shared silence that seeped into them both as they sat precariously on a cliff edge.

25

Shipwright • Saer llongau • Sanie alsufun

EMRYS WAS DRAWN TO the boat, his hands feeling the way like a blind man. He let his fingers move over her surface, relying on instincts and old, old memories, the ones that were old enough not to have left him. He had been a shipwright, a maker of vessels. Efa watched him as his whole body became transfixed by the boat.

He knew her, too, had worked on her with Nefyn's father. Had perfected her lines, her balance. They had used some wood from a successful boat that they had finished breaking to bring her good fortune. Emrys greeted her warmly, like an old lover, his palms conducting a holy communion. He smiled as he took the damage in, her age, her weakened surfaces, and Efa felt a pang of something akin to loss as she watched him.

'Do you think you can make her seaworthy?' Hamza asked. Emrys smiled.

'Nothing is worthy of the sea,' he replied, 'but I can make her sail again.' His eyes were drawn to the timbers in the boatshed roof and the tools in the boxes.

Hamza watched him. Followed his thinking. Emrys continued, 'We'll need oil. Diesel. And when we've finished, we'll need the highest tide possible.' He looked out of the boatshed door towards the sea.

He hadn't been to the cove since they brought the boat back here. A couple of men from the village had been sent to recover it, to bring it home, as was tradition. It would be up to the dead fisherman's son if he wanted to repair her or not. He had sailed in her, too. On her maiden voyage, as a friend and as an engineer. And later, when he had some time off from the harbour-side, he would sometimes be invited to go fishing. He didn't have a boat of his own, as he always used the ones in for repair, so he would welcome the nod to join the fishermen or Nefyn's father now and again.

He had seen him, in fact, pulling Nefyn's mother from the sea. Had been with him. He had always per-suaded himself that she had swum too far out. She had with her only a cloak. She wasn't making much sense. It must have been the heat; it had been such a hot sum-mer. He tried to talk to Alun, the twins' father, about it later, told him of his surprise that she was living with him. He was threatened into silence, didn't dare ask about the bruises on her arms when, sometimes, she came to bring Alun his lunch. His cheeks burned with the shame of it, but that's how it was back then; they weren't very different to many other couples and they all had to work together in the small harbour village. He turned to look at Hamza.

'It will take a couple of weeks,' Emrys said.

Hamza nodded.

'I will help you.'

Efa smiled at them uncertainly. She had been scared to bring him. He had been so unsettled recently but she knew he would be able to help and for a moment, watching him, she saw him come alive. They had been taking their leave for years. Each month a new loss. The talks they used to have after supper. The way he brought her tea in the morning. The irony of the fact that he had always had a much better memory than her for the things they had done, the places they had been. She watched him, a new leaving in his eyes. It was as if someone had shone a light on a path for him in the darkness, and, grateful for the direction, he seemed eager to begin his journey.

'Can he do it?' Nefyn was standing waiting for him. Her voice startled Hamza as he closed the door behind him.

'Yes.'

'How long will it take?'

Hamza shrugged. 'A couple of weeks.'

Nefyn nodded. She had watched him last night. Restless once again in his sleep. Nefyn had sensed him getting up in the middle of the night. Had heard the door opening. She had got up herself and looked out at the cliff-top. She had seen Hamza pray. Asking the night if someone was there. He had prayed like a child. Diligently. Honestly. Uncynically. A sense that anything was possible. Nefyn had watched as he raised his head once again and listened to the sound of the waves reverberating in the cove below.

When he had returned to the house, she had lit the fire. He had made some coffee and they had sat exchanging stories, some from Nefyn's childhood, some from Hamza's. Each story drawing the other near. Hamza telling her of how, when he was a child, his family had time to enjoy each other's company, to recount stories.

How they had always been told, rather than written down, changing as they moved through the mouths and the minds of their tellers. Nefyn told him the things her mother had said of the sea. How windows on the deep would sometimes open for a few chosen fishermen, how sometimes they would come across smooth patches of sea, mirror-like and clear, revealing cities on the seabed and winding rivers. Glimpses into another world. They talked in this way, each common theme warming another, until dawn infused their words with light. After that, they had become silent. Both their thoughts centring on the boat, on its repair, and on their imminent separation.

This morning, Nefyn had followed Hamza to the cliff edge but had been unable to follow him down to the cove, the reality of his return home resting on her heavily. She had turned back and waited for him. Now Nefyn watched as he took his seat by the fire.

'It could happen,' he said quietly. 'I had hoped . . . but . . . it seemed *so* far away.'

Nefyn moved towards him. He took her hand, studied it, and then he pulled her down into his lap. Felt the nape of her neck with his fingers. Her hair over his face.

'Two weeks,' she whispered, but he silenced her. Her lips cold under his, her taste invoking a thirst in him that he had not known was there.

26

Map ◆ Kharita ◆ Map

THE WORLD HAD FALLEN away. The only sound was the rain on the roof tiles, its gentle rhythm a reminder of life outside. He had laid her down. Closed his eyes and felt for her. He had seen primitive maps carved from wood, each indent a cove, a secret place, so that sailors could navigate at night under the stars. He understood them now as he began to know the tilt of her collarbone, the jut of her thigh. Her body at once ordinary and extraordinary. He had pressed her close, tasted her, but she was still unknowable. Like water somehow. She had studied him. Eyes open in the dark, her fingers entwined in his hair. Afterwards they had been silent, listening to the world turn.

When the rain stopped, they made their way outside to the bench where Nefyn seemed happiest. Hamza lit the inky sky with a hurricane lamp which illuminated the old floats hanging there in nets, like stained glass. Their reflections revealing a crescent moon, the stubborn stars. Nefyn sat, her legs across his lap, her mind far away.

'I waited for you,' she said eventually, 'all those years.'

Hamza laid his head back, felt the warmth of her legs under his palms. Nefyn studied his face.

'I knew you'd come.'

Hamza smiled. He thought about the sea, about

the strandline. About the life he once lived. The words got caught in his throat. Nefyn watched him think.

'Fatima, my wife, she died.' He laughed bitterly. 'No, my wife, Fatima, she was killed. Buying food. A stray bullet. It wasn't meant for her.' His voice had deepened now.

'There was no sound, no one even noticed. She just dropped her bag. Slid to the floor.'

His face was drenched with the lamplight. 'By the time I got there, they had taken her away. And I did not know how to feel. How can you feel something like that?'

Nefyn's eyes darkened with tears. She reached out for his shoulder. Let her hand rest there. The lamp spluttered a moment, casting shadows around them, the ever-present sea murmuring below.

'You see, I was so angry, so full of rage ...' His voice trailed off. 'I tried to carry on working, but every day, things became worse. You must understand, the regime killed my wife, they controlled my job, they were watching everything, listening.' He stopped talking a moment, cleared his throat. 'And every night Hussein would ask for stories, but I had none. I was sick, sick of it, and then the allies, they approached me. A General Reeves. Wanted me to help them. Their maps weren't good enough, they weren't accurate enough. So, I helped them. They trusted me, and I put my faith in them. My brother, my family, they warned me. They said people knew, that the regime would find out, but I didn't care. After Fatima, I wanted to do anything. Anything on Earth that would stop the war, make the whole thing come to an end ...' He let out another bitter laugh. 'They'd planned an attack, Reeves and his men. The allies were training the Kurdish fighters, they were working undercover. I'd given them the maps, helped them understand the terrain, but they were ambushed. Twelve men killed.' He looked downwards now. His voice becoming strangled as he dragged the words out into the open. Pulled them out in front of Nefyn. 'I helped them for two years, I trusted them, but when it came to it, they didn't have faith in me. They couldn't trust me back. They called me a traitor. Thought I knew too much about what they had planned. They could have killed me, but they decided perhaps I would be more useful alive . . . be able to tell them things.' Hamza's eyes rolled back and his breath grew short as he relived the horror. His face was glistening with tears. He pushed them away angrily. 'I promise you, I did not know that they would die.'

Nefyn listened to him weep. She sat with him. Close. Her hand still on his shoulder, feeling Hamza's grief fall gently upon her like a cloak. She sat in silence until she heard the whisper of dusty wings. Some moths fluttered at the lamp, their silvery bodies drawn to the light. Hungry for its warmth. Nefyn watched them. Memories summoned from the darkness. Flickering. Hamza turned to look at her. 'They took away my name, my freedom, my life . . . everything.' His eyes were wide in the half-light. 'You see,' he confessed, 'I don't exist.'

Nefyn reached out her fingers, pressed their backs on to his face. Held one of his dark curls. Smoothed it in her fingertips.

'It's all right,' she said softly, her voice thick with tears, 'neither do I.'

The rain began again. Falling in heavy, glassy droplets around them. Nefyn turned her attention skywards and, as she did, they stopped in mid-air. Thousands upon thousands of droplets hung above them, defying gravity and the laws of the Earth herself. Hamza looked on in wonder as they glistened gold and silver in the marine-blue sky.

27

Confession ✦ *Cyfaddefiad* ✦ *Aietiraf*

EFA HAD DIALLED THE number that Hamza gave her.
Hamza could not be moved from the cottage and
they had agreed together that if the military were
tracking calls, it would be safer to use Efa as an inter-
mediary. She had listened to the long dial tone. The
voice answering hundreds of miles away. Her accent.
His accent. Their common words. The incredulity.
The things that Hamza had told her to say to convince
him that Hamza was still alive. His colleague's silence.
The sound of shouting names in a language she didn't
understand. A woman crying. Efa had listened, her
hand on Emrys's arm. The exchange of numbers. She
had told them about the boat. She had tried to write
everything down correctly.

This morning, she had left Emrys with Hamza.
He was sleeping well these days, the exhaustion of
working on the boat weighing heavily on his frail body.
She had kept him at home the day before, fearing it
was becoming too much for him. Hamza did all the
heavy lifting, of course, but the effort of concentration
was difficult for Emrys. Efa would keep out of the village until she collected Emrys at the end of the day in
order not to arouse suspicions, particularly from Mary
next door, who would surely notice he wasn't with her
and ask questions.

Today, she had called in at the church. She did not

know why. She had pushed the door open. Felt for the keys in her pocket, wondering whether she should sweep out the sand once more, when she saw him in the front pew, his head bent over. He hadn't moved when she approached, as she sat beside him. Waited. Listening to the sea far away. She saw a slight movement of his head. He knew it was her.

'I don't know what to do,' he whispered. His voice clouded in the cold church. Efa didn't answer until eventually he sat back, his face drawn, pale. Defeated. Joseph's eyes were searching the cross above the altar.

'Do you know what it's like to live in . . .' He paused. 'To not understand the person you live with, the person you love? To wonder every day what they could do?'

Efa waited, seeing in Joseph's eyes a deep sadness.

'You should have seen the way our mother looked at her. It was like I was invisible.'

Efa's cheeks flushed, as she was guilty of this as much as anyone. It was as if she had always looked over Joseph's shoulder, searching for Nefyn. Her absence making her more present. Efa shrugged contritely 'We've all got brothers and sisters, that's what happens.'

'No.' He shook his head, his jaw setting. 'Not like her.'

A coldness crept up Efa's spine. She had heard the stories, of course. The things Emrys sometimes said in his sleep. The way the memories seemed to resurface over and over in his failing mind. Efa fumbled for the words. Careful.

'Is she . . .' She thought for a moment. 'I always

thought about your mother, that there was something different about her . . . Is . . . is Nefyn the same?' Efa tried to control the trembling in her body. Tried to look ahead. As if his answer made no difference to her. As if it would be mundane.

'Yes,' he said simply.

Efa knew. She already knew. Her own father had told her the stories. About them. How they sometimes intermarried. How they were unknowable.

'It's like . . .' he continued, 'it's like she holds her breath on land.'

Efa felt her neck and chest prickle.

'If they find her . . .' Joseph rubbed his face with his palms, left the implications to Efa to fathom. Efa's thoughts turned. Her mind busy.

'You see, she killed someone.'

Efa's eyes snapped up to his face.

'Made him walk into the sea. I told . . . I told him, a guard, where Hamza was . . . he went to find him and she made him walk into the sea.'

Efa took this in for a moment.

'She made him?'

'She . . . she . . . He just walked into the sea.'

Efa thought of Nefyn's mother. Her loyalty to her. Her needing to be accepted as clean. As clear of sin. The silent promise she had made to herself to look after the children.

'If they're looking for him,' she began, 'the best way to protect her is to help him.' Joseph exhaled noisily. 'Think about it.' She turned her body to face him. 'Nobody knows the cove like you do. Nobody knows how to navigate the sea. The watchtowers.'

He shook his head. 'Joseph? Do you want to protect her?'

He nodded.

'Then, it's the only way.'

Joseph took in her words. Tried to arrange them so that they made sense to him.

'With your help, he'll get away quicker.'

They sat for a moment. One thinking about the impossibility of what she had just heard. The other about the impossibility of what he must do.

Owens's bloated body came in at the tide's insistence. The sea had tried for several days to offer him up and, on the third day, it had succeeded. He was found, slack-jawed and sunken-eyed, south of the harbour, by a man sent out of the house by his wife to smoke. The police had arrived and cordoned the place off.

The Lieutenant Colonel had already received news of a body having been found before the meeting that morning. A meeting he chaired with more good humour than usual. The matter finally closed, he waved through measures that had been festering on the agenda with a rejuvenated sense of optimism. They would move the Unmanned Aerial Drones to Portsmouth. From there, they would be deployed overseas. He was just dressing for his black-tie dinner at the seniors' mess when the second call came through. The body had been removed and although it was too early to assume anything officially and to establish an identity, the body was definitely that of a Caucasian male, fair-haired, and young. Certainly not Middle Eastern. He was also wearing military clothing. The Lieutenant Colonel thanked the DCI. Put down the phone, felt his shoulders crackle with tension and swore profusely under his breath.

28

Luck ✦ Lwc ✦ Hadh

Nefyn watched Hamza as he studied the fire. He and Emrys had worked on the boat all day. Efa had promised to go to the old stores by the harbour-master's office, to which Emrys still had a key, to collect some parts, and they were making progress. The boat had started to come alive. Hamza watched as Emrys pressed his hands on her, felt her potential. The broken mast held a secret. At its base, as they removed it, they uncovered the silver coin placed there by Nefyn's father to bring the boat luck. Hamza had brought it home for Nefyn, and she sat feeling its weight in her palm as they listened to the fire.

Old women used to press silver coins into her hand when she was a very small child. Nefyn remembered that. It was one of her earliest memories. Hiding in her mother's skirts as they'd crouch down and place the cool heavy discs on her palm for luck. They seemed to know at their age that knowledge and learning wouldn't be enough. That the path any child took would be treacherous. The coin warmed in Nefyn's palm.

'Efa said that Khalid called her house,' said Hamza, looking over at her. 'They're doing everything they can to find Hussein.' Nefyn nodded. Considered the quiet fear in Hamza's words. 'She said they'll call her with any more news.' Hamza looked down now, his thoughts turning inwards. 'I thought I would know if he was still alive, be able to *feel* it. But I don't.' He paused for a moment, looked up at Nefyn. 'You know, I held him, when he was first born. Covered in blood. Down. His legs, they were curled . . . folded . . . still in the shape of the womb.'

Nefyn smiled.

'His skin.' Hamza smiled, thinking of its beauty.

Nefyn felt the warmth of his words, looked down at the coin and turned it in her fingers. Studied its two faces.

'You know, there are children. In camps. Who do not know who they are. What or where their country was . . . living this . . .'

'Half-life?' suggested Nefyn.

'Yes. War is their whole story.'

Nefyn shuffled off the chair. Went to sit on the blanket on the floor beside him. Rested her head on his shoulder.

'You'll find him.'

Hamza closed his eyes. Put his hand over Nefyn's. A sudden fear overwhelming him.

'Come with me,' he said.

Nefyn smiled. He opened his eyes. Turned to face her.

'You can't stay here. Not with Joseph.'

He pushed her hair behind her ear. Nefyn caught his hand, laid it on her lap. Looked at it. Shook her head.

'But why?'

'I can't leave.'

'We could find a house. By the sea. We could find Hussein. We could be together.'

Nefyn let him talk.

'We could hide away and no one would know.'

Nefyn placed her hand over his mouth, her eyes darkening with tears.

'Stop,' she said, her voice tight in her throat, 'stop.'

Then he held her. Closed his eyes. Nefyn stared over his shoulder, her dark eyes wide.

'It's a good story,' she said.

'Yes,' he said, his voice deep, 'yes, it is.'

The report clearly stated that Owens must have entered the water in the three-mile range south of the military base. His next of kin had been informed. The most likely point of entry into the water was a small cove. No trauma injuries or sign of a fall or an attack were found, suggesting that the most likely cause of death was suicide. The toxicology report noted substantial levels of alcohol and marijuana, which would have hastened his death and made swimming more difficult.

The Lieutenant Colonel had read the report and closed the file. He sat, his hands spread palms down on the table in front of him, before calling the DCI to ask him to make discreet enquiries at any properties near the cove. They should ask whether anyone had seen anything. If anyone had been in contact with the deceased before he had entered the water.

Within a couple of hours, two police officers had been dispatched. They took the winding coastal road out of the village. They parked, and walked the path into the cove. It was getting dark, and there was nothing to see. They looked into the boatshed, too. Some tools. Ongoing work on an old boat, nothing that you wouldn't expect to see on the coast. By the time they reached the top of the path once more, they were both breathing hard. They looked towards the small cottage balancing on the cliff.

Inside, Hamza and Nefyn lay in front of the fire, fast asleep and entwined in each other. The prospect of being separated had exhausted them. Hamza's sense of home had been complicated by Nefyn. He had lain as she slept in his arms knowing that he could not leave her to her brother. That he could not leave her to live under siege.

By the time the policemen knocked on the cottage door, it was late. Nefyn and Hamza awoke to their shouting. He placed a hand on her mouth. They froze, wide-eyed. They both knew the door wasn't locked. Male voices. They lay still, knowing that they would be shielded from view under the window. They listened as someone tested the door. Tried the handle. Felt it move. Fear prickled through them both. Then, a third voice joined the conversation. The door handle sprang back up. Nefyn knew the voice immediately. He asked them what they were doing. Where their papers were. Hamza turned towards Nefyn. One word. That's all it would take. Nefyn pressed her face into the crook of Hamza's neck. A conversation. It was his boat. Yes. He was a fisherman. Yes. What had it to do with them? Only his sister. They could take a look if they wanted to. No. He hadn't seen anyone around. The front door opened. She wasn't right. He was her carer. He was calling her. Nefyn looked up sharply. Hamza urged her to go. Go. She got up. Walked towards the doorway. A muffled conversation.

'Nefyn?' His voice impatient now. The officers reassuring him that it wasn't necessary to see her. 'Nefyn!'

She stood in the doorway. They hardly looked at her they were so embarrassed.

'It's OK,' they said.

She looked at the floor.

'Are you happy now?' Joseph asked. They apologized for taking up so much of his time, and Nefyn stood watching them leave. Joseph nodded his head to them before closing the door behind them. He held his palm against it a moment, before turning to look at his sister and Hamza.

29

Llwybr ✦ *Route* ✦ *Tariq*

JOSEPH STOOD BY THE door, his eyes averted, as if simultaneously caught and surrendering. His denim jacket looked too big for him. The bluster he had shown the policemen dissipated. His shoulders tight and high. His face thin.

'Don't look at me like that, Joseph,' Nefyn said.

'Like what?'

'You're scared.'

'I'm not scared, I—'

'You're scared,' she interjected.

His jaw tightened. He turned his eyes towards her. His voice small and tight. He waited a moment.

'I saw what you did.'

Nefyn's voice was steady. 'I know you did.'

'It was me,' he said. 'I was the one who told him where he was.'

Nefyn watched him.

'I know,' she said.

'It was my fault.'

Nefyn shook her head. 'It was no one's fault.'

'So what are you going to do?'

Joseph spread his arms. A gesture of surrender. He looked away, incapable of locking eyes with her for long. Nefyn's head tilted to the side.

'Are you scared of *me*, Joseph?'

Nefyn heard Hamza retreat to the kitchen. Leaving

them alone. Joseph looked at her. Her eyes filled. 'What do you think I'll do? You're my brother. We were born into this together.'

He shook his head. '*You* were born into this.'

'No, *we* were both born into this.'

'I'm not like you!' His voice was raised now.

'What am I like, Joseph?'

He rubbed his head. His back against the door.

'What am I like, Joseph? Say it!'

'No!'

'Why?' Nefyn laughed. A bitter silence settling between them.

'You lied to me about Efa. You said she couldn't be trusted. You lied to me about those pills.'

'No.'

'You lied to me.'

Joseph rounded on her. 'Do you know what they'd do to you if they found you? Do you have any idea of how cruel they can be?' His voice was rising now. 'You've not seen it! You've not felt it! Do you know what they do to people who are different? You have no idea.'

'You said you were looking after me.'

'I was!'

'You said—'

'You wouldn't last a minute in the real world. It's me who has to work, me who has to work things out.'

Nefyn looked at him. He looked like he had always done as a boy. Spiteful. Sheepish. Brotherly. His eyes dropped. His voice softened and, suddenly, his face crumpled.

'I saw you, collecting things. Your things from the

sea. Precious things. Looking after them. I was just doing the same.'

Joseph looked up, his countenance open now. His eyes luminous with tears. Nefyn watched him carefully.

'I was keeping you safe, Nefyn.'

'But that couldn't last, could it?' she said.

Joseph shook his head. He looked at her. Her face had filled out. Her skin whiter somehow, a contrast to her hair. So similar to their mother.

'I don't want to lose you, Nefyn.' His eyes were darkening now as he searched her face. 'You're all I've got left.'

It was dark now, save for the muted light in the kitchen. His features looked softer, too, and they stood for a moment until she felt Hamza come to stand in the doorframe behind her. The tempering of Joseph's voice drawing him nearer. Joseph looked away. Shrugged away his confession as if it were nothing.

'Joseph—' Nefyn began.

'I can help him,' he cut across her, his embarrassment sharpening his words.

He looked up, looked at Hamza standing behind Nefyn, his hands on her arms. He looked towards the floor again. His posture defeated.

'I can help him. If that's what you want.'

Joseph spread the maps on the kitchen table. They marked the military base as well as the smaller lookout points along the coast. The sea was open, the few

154

fishing vessels left in the bay allowed to sail within a certain area of The Range now that the main testing was over. This would all make it easier for them. Joseph used a protractor to measure the angles between the lookouts, tracking an invisible course. They would need to exploit their blind spots. There were enough of them; the local fishermen had used them over the years when they absolutely had to, but no one had tried to navigate out of the cove and across the Irish Sea through The Range unseen. Joseph had contacts in the North, friends who worked on vessels carrying shipping containers from Liverpool to France. They passed every day. If they could get Hamza out to a certain point in the Irish Sea, they could offload him on the quiet on to one of the boats bound for France.

If they went out before dawn, they'd catch the highest tide, there'd be fewer soldiers manning the watch points and they could use Joseph's sextant to find their way, and remain digitally undetected. That way, they'd have enough light to see the horizon and enough darkness to be guided by the stars. Polaris and Vega would give them their bearings and they would work it out from there. Hamza nodded. The spring tide would be in their favour, as the moon loomed closest to Earth. They had a week's worth of work left on the boat, and if everything came together, they could be ready by the highest tide.

'Thank you,' said Hamza. Joseph found it difficult to look at him. Nefyn cleared the table and Hamza helped her lay it with bread and cheese, and they sat to eat. Nefyn raised her eyes every now and again to watch them. Hamza caught her and looked over at

Joseph, the tension in his body worsening now that his practical input was over. Then he brushed his hands on his trousers, got up to leave.

'Please don't,' said Hamza. 'I can sleep out there, you go to your bed.'

Joseph shook his head.

'No, it's better if we stick to how things are. Don't change anything for now.'

Joseph turned for the door, before hearing Hamza's voice behind him.

'Joseph?' He turned to see Hamza pulling his lost phone from his pocket and offering it to him. A tentativeness in Hamza's eyes.

'I'm sorry,' he said uncertainly, 'I didn't know what to do.'

Joseph studied him a moment, the mistrust between them dissipating. 'It's OK. I understand.' He pocketed the phone. 'I'll bring it back to you; you'll need it when you sail.' Hamza nodded.

Nefyn followed him to the door. It was dark outside, the moon invisible under rain clouds. Cold. Nefyn held the door open. Waited as he passed her.

'Thank you,' she said, her words loud in the silence. Joseph nodded. He lingered a moment. Looked out to sea. He opened his mouth to say something, but his words failed him. He nodded again, turned and walked away, and Nefyn watched him go.

30

Cantre'r Gwaelod • Drowned City • Medina Maghmoura

'H AMZA?' NEFYN KISSED THE side of his face. 'Wake up.' It was dark. Pitch-black.

'Come, come with me.' Her face was inches above his, pale. A soft smile. He got up. Dressed hurriedly, walked to the living room, but she was already gone, the door left open for him.

'Nefyn?' He pulled on his shoes and followed.

It was still, the sound of the sea seemingly far away. As her figure disappeared from the cliff-top down towards the cove, he followed, dreamlike, listening to her footsteps and her laughter. He stumbled half asleep down the path, bracing against the drop with his thighs, steadying himself with his outstretched arms. The path was becoming second nature, the obstacle it had once been felt incomprehensible to him now.

'Nefyn,' he whispered, having reached the bottom. She was walking out to sea. His feet clacked on the stones as he followed her. It was a clear night, the moon waxing ready for its spring fullness, lacing every stone with silver. The sea whispered in the distance, the tide further out than he had ever seen it. His feet suddenly silent on sand. He had hit the tidemark.

Nefyn continued to walk out until dark shapes started forming under the moon. The sand riven with the ghost of the tide, ridged and uneven beneath his feet.

His foot caught on a serpentine shape. Sinewy and dark. He gasped. Looked for Nefyn, but she was nowhere to be seen. He focused his eyes through the gloom to see dark shapes rising all around him. Twisted, their limbs reaching, cleaving, uncovered by the low tide.

'Nefyn?' His voice disappeared with the breeze.

He looked around, more and more shapes coming into view. Nefyn had vanished. The sound of the sea louder now, insistent, as if about to turn. He approached one of the figures, put out his hand. Touched its smooth surface. And as the moon lit up the seabed for a moment, he saw the floor of the ocean littered with them. Then, a soft voice behind him.

'It's a forest,' she said. Nefyn in the moonlight. Her eyes alive. 'A few times a year, the tide recedes far enough.'

Hamza was short of breath.

'These are trees?'

Nefyn smiled.

'Thousands and thousands of years old.' Nefyn looked around. 'From another time, another place.' She gazed up at them. 'This place used to be someone's home. Someone's shelter.' She walked towards him, rested the side of her face on his chest so she could listen to his heart. 'My mother brought me here as a child. She'd make me listen. And I could hear them. All the people who had lived here. Died here. They never disappeared.'

Hamza smiled. The dark trees breathing around them.

'Everything changes, but their lives became rooted here. Became part of this place. Untouchable.' Nefyn looked up at him. 'Even if places, countries are hard to see, even if they seem to disappear in front of your eyes, they're still there. I just wanted you to know that,' she whispered. 'I wanted you to feel that.'

Hamza looked at her, his eyes filling. He wrapped his arms around her and they stood in the submerged forest, listening, until the tide finally started to turn.

The Captain was unable to sleep, switched on the bedside lamp in his quarters. He made himself some coffee and headed to his office, nodding here and there to the soldiers on duty. It wasn't his meeting with the Lieutenant Colonel that was playing on his mind per se, but a niggling memory of their last dealings with Owens. He was sure he had heard the Lieutenant Colonel say to him that his record was exemplary. They were duty-bound to investigate any case of suicide within the army and when he pulled up his paperwork, the memory and the evidence just did not tally. He unlocked the door of his office, clicked on his table lamp and waited for the bulb to illuminate the gloom.

He may have misheard, of course – these things were not impossible – but there was something in the rather erratic behaviour of the Lieutenant Colonel recently that unsettled him. He knew that they had had a meeting not long before Owens walked into the sea. A meeting that the Captain hadn't been party to. He pulled up Owens's record once again. It wouldn't be hard for him to look into the incidents he found there, but he risked offending the Lieutenant Colonel if he caught wind of it. After all, filing a complaint against a senior officer could tarnish your own record even if it transpired that the complaint was justified. He threw down the record once again and sat back in his chair.

There was something about Owens. It was impossible to generalize, or to know what state of mind anyone was in, but he just didn't strike the Captain as someone who would do that. He was a survivor, an opportunist. And most opportunists would try to find a way. He was resourceful, clever, and had had the audacity to challenge his superiors. This was unusual, and showed a remarkable sense of self-worth.

He sighed. Looked at the clock. It was three thirty in the morning.

The Captain had served under enough senior officers to know they were human, fallible, but it was another thing to cast aspersions on someone's honesty. He had resigned himself several times over the last few days to forgetting about it. The matter was closed, the toxicology irrefutable. But still. It was a pity about Prisoner B, a somewhat strange act of God, but this, this death felt altogether more human. He gave another deep sigh and stretched out his arms, before getting up and walking to the window. The sea was far away tonight, a heavy moon, the barracks silent and dark. It was difficult to find silence here. In confined quarters, there was always someone to interrupt your thoughts. Time to yourself was so rare, and even then, leisure was usually taken with colleagues. He opened the window for a moment. Let the breeze in and contemplated the laughable smallness of the barracks perched on the cliff edge under the darkening moon.

Gogledd • North • Shamal

J OSEPH LET HIMSELF OUT of the house by the harbour as the morning mists cleared. He walked past the deserted jetty, listening to the bows of the boats jostling in the water. It was almost imperceptible, but he could feel the first indications of spring in the breeze. He would walk out of the village early, and up towards the main road north. From there he would hitch-hike to the run-down town by the docks. Make some enquiries. Pull in some favours. He knew some of the crane operators up there. Had drunk with them in seedy bars by the sea. Played cards. Lost the little money they had. His legs pulled as he walked upwards out of the village.

Nefyn looked different with Hamza. He had been thinking about it the night before as he lay in the narrow bed. She had a liveliness about her, a fearlessness that he hadn't seen since they were children. When their mother was around, Nefyn could be provocative, bold. Would tease her father about storms and deep seas. She'd look up into their mother's eyes then, search there for judgement, which she never found. Their father would take a belt to Joseph for being headstrong, but he never did the same to Nefyn. Their father said it was because she was a girl, but Joseph knew that it was much more than that. He knew their mother was powerless against him, but Joseph felt that maybe he was playing it careful with Nefyn. He had never seen her turn on their father, but she wasn't afraid of him, and their mother loved that about her. As she grew, she became bolder still, would speak up for her mother. Walk to stand in the room if there was ever an altercation. Watch him. Her face still. Her ability to unsettle him growing as her face bore more and more resemblance to their mother's.

It had all changed one day when their father was out at sea. Joseph was sent to the village on some errands, and when he came back the cottage was empty. He waited there all day, alone. He called for his mother, but there was no sign of her, or of Nefyn. As dusk fell, he had made his way to the cove only to find his sister prostrate on the tideline, her eight-year-old body heavy with shock, her hair in waves around her. She wouldn't speak. He had asked her over and over where their mother was but she couldn't answer.

He had carried her then, although not much stronger than her. Hoisted her on to his back, bent forward to bring her up to the cottage, the fear making his body cold and setting off a quivering in the pit of his stomach. He had laid her down, put a blanket over her. Their father, when he had come home, had searched the cottage, searched the cove, his eyes wild, and swearing. He had shaken Nefyn by her shoulders, shouted at her to speak, to tell him where her mother was, but she had refused or been unable to answer. What was clear was that she was gone and that was when the light went out of Nefyn's eyes. She didn't challenge their father any more. She became quiet and when they went rock-pooling together, she would sit looking away, as if part of her had already left.

Joseph felt their mother's absence as a wound inflicted. And his anger had grown with the years until he had gone down to the sea sometimes and spat and raged at it. Love wasn't enough. Their mother had shown him that. The bond that she had with them meant nothing. Blood was thinner than water. He had even felt for their father, as one night he woke and sat in his vest outside their parents' room listening to him sob. Heard him explaining to acquaintances that his wife had left. Helped him clear all her things from the cottage, piling up her clothes outside the house and setting it all on fire. Watching as the soot and the sparks were carried over the dark sea by the wind, and the embers sickened on the floor.

Joseph turned once again and continued his way towards the main road. Hamza had to leave, he knew that. Once that was done, then they would find a new way forward.

❧

Emrys was tiring. Hamza could sense it in the hesitancy of his hands, the smile he gave when he was buying time to think. They had been working on the boat all morning and she was so very near completion. Only the water would be able to test her, of course, but Emrys was happy and that was good enough for Hamza.

'Come,' he said to Emrys, touching his arm gently, 'you need to rest.' Emrys looked at him a moment, nodded. Hamza sat down, gestured to Emrys to do the same. He opened the flask of black tea that Nefyn had given him. Listened as the stopper opened, and the steam curled into the air. He poured two enamel mugs as Emrys sighed his way on to the upturned oil barrel. Hamza handed him the cup and they listened a while to the gulls carousing over the cove. Black-headed and common, all swirling in the air as if enlivened by the change of temperature that was coming.

'She was very beautiful,' Emrys said, clearing his throat. His voice had become threadbare in recent years, Efa had noticed it. It came from the top of his chest, as his lungs had become shallower. She had often wondered whether his voice was leaving him too. Hamza looked at the boat.

'She still is.'

Emrys smiled.

'I mean Arianell.'

Hamza's brow furrowed.

'I'm sorry, I don't understand.'

'I meant. I'm sorry . . .' Emrys searched a moment for an explanation, names. 'Nefyn's mother, Arianell.'

'I didn't know you knew her.'

'Efa and I both did.'

His hands were veined, large, the skin paper-thin, littered with sun marks, just like his grandfather's. 'My grandmother told me stories, when I was a child. About them. How they were different.'

Hamza listened. Warming his hands on his mug.

'When I was growing up I thought it was because they wanted to scare us. Keep us away from the sea.' Hamza smiled. 'Arianell was like . . . a light . . . you couldn't help but turn towards her. I have never seen Nefyn. Is she the same?'

Hamza thought about her, drew her near in his mind.

'Yes, she is.'

Emrys cleared his throat once more; he was coughing more these days, as if he couldn't quite take a full breath.

'Tell me,' Emrys asked, 'are you a religious man?'

Hamza considered.

'I was. Then I wasn't.' His mind flitted back to a brick cell. Four walls. His brow furrowed. 'I thought I had lost wonder. I thought I would never feel it again . . . but I have . . .'

Emrys studied his face. Interested. Intense.

'Efa always tried to take me to that church,' confided Emrys, 'but my Mass was being with the sea. It felt closer to me.'

Hamza smiled, but Emrys seemed preoccupied, the window of clarity on his mind sharp.

'I haven't got much time left.'

'Now come,' Hamza cajoled.

'Don't, I like you too much for you to lie to me.'

Hamza's smile faltered; he felt the weight of his words.

The old man continued, 'You know, I think you have five or six moments in your life, where time . . . when you are connected to something bigger.' Emrys's eyes were damp. A clarity there that Hamza hadn't seen before. 'I felt it with Efa, when we were young, that moment when you can't love someone more. And I could feel inside me everyone who was alive and everyone who had ever lived who had felt that way.' Emrys's hands were shaking now. 'We never had children, so I can't talk about that, but I felt it once when I was at sea. It was dark. The engine failed and I was alone. I looked out, and the sea was like glass. Not a whisper of wind. Its vastness. My smallness. And I felt everyone's loneliness. Everyone in the world. It is those moments. Seconds. Fleeting.' His voice quietened. 'You see, those moments are the length of our lives.' He looked up at Hamza, eyes glittering. 'I am glad she brings you wonder,' he said again.

Hamza smiled, and a comfortable silence fell between them. 'The ones from the sea.' He was out of breath now. 'They know things, you know.'

Hamza looked at him, a question forming on his lips.

'I don't know what you mean?'

'They know more things than you and I ever could.' His eyes were fading. Hamza could see that. He was exhausted. 'They can do things. That other people can't.'

Hamza nodded. Emrys lowered his voice again. 'They say they have power over life and death and the thin thread in between.'

Hamza listened to his words, took in the weight of them. He watched as Emrys slowly pulled himself up to standing. Brushed himself off and walked towards the boat. Hamza sat looking straight ahead, his body suddenly cold.

32

Favour • Ffafr • Muhabaa

THE LIEUTENANT COLONEL WAS apoplectic, the Captain could see that. It was in his every movement, the set of his jaw. He gestured for him to enter his office, could barely bring himself to sit down. He nodded to the chair. The Captain sat.

'I guess you know what this is about,' the Lieutenant Colonel said through gritted teeth.

'Yes, sir.'

He was still standing, the heat of his anger raging through him.

'I can't begin to understand what possessed you.'

The Captain didn't answer. He sat trying not to look defeated. His posture neutral.

Passive.

'What have you got to say for yourself?'

'I'm afraid the records I saw don't match the original records for this particular soldier. I couldn't overlook that, and I shouldn't be asked to.'

The Lieutenant Colonel studied him, squeezing his hands on the back of his chair, his back bent.

'The investigations team is arriving tomorrow.'

The Captain kept quiet.

'You know how close to the completion of this project we are, and what this could do to my record, even when I'm proven innocent?'

The Captain sat impassive as the older man looked at him, changed tack. Sat down.

'I thought we were friends?'

'We're colleagues, sir.'

'I've helped you out God knows how many times.'

'And for that I thank you, but I couldn't turn a blind eye to this, particularly when a man has committed suicide. The circumstances around that have to be investigated and any anomalies addressed.'

The Lieutenant Colonel had held his post at the barracks since before the Captain arrived. He could tell that he was privately educated, one of the boys, but still, he seemed pleasant enough. He had invited him for dinner several times but the Captain rarely seemed to have a gap in his diary. He knew he was ambitious, of course, but he hadn't thought he'd be quite so inflexible. The Lieutenant Colonel lowered his voice.

'Listen, perhaps you made a mistake, mistook his record for someone with a similar name. It's easily done.'

The Captain looked up.

'What you're asking me to do is illegal.'

'What I'm asking you to do is be decent. I didn't touch that soldier. I don't know why he did what he did but it was nothing to do with me.'

'Then you have nothing to worry about,' the Captain rebutted.

'Do you know how hard I've worked to get where I am?'

'Yes, sir.'

'What you're doing is undermining everything I've worked for. There'll be a full investigation into the workings of this barracks, so I'd make pretty sure if I were you that my nose was clean too.'

The Captain raised one eyebrow.

'Are you threatening me?'

'Of course not.'

The Captain's face hardened.

'I'm glad to hear it.' He got up. 'I understand you'll be on a little gardening leave whilst some enquiries are made.'

'It seems so.'

'Then I'll look forward to seeing you back when all this is . . . resolved.'

Joseph sat at the bar, waiting. It was an old pub, ramshackle. Cheap beer for men who worked at the docks. Cardboard neon stars displaying prices. His friend arrived, and he got up wordlessly to buy him a drink before they came back to sit down. This man would be the first in a chain. He worked at the shipping yard, loading containers on to ships. In order to get what Joseph needed, he would need him to make a deal with his friends who worked the ships. The ones who stayed at the same low-end B&Bs by the quayside, away from their families for weeks on end. They would have to coordinate timings and tides, and stopping a container ship was nigh on impossible. All this would cost. And there were no guarantees. No one would want to take too many risks either; work was scarce and any of this reaching management would be a disaster. They wouldn't put him into a container, but would have to pass him off as crew on the other side, all of which would take some doing.

He laughed at him to begin with. Shook his head. Then Joseph told him a little about his story, how they'd get one over on the authorities if they helped him.

'How much you got?'

Joseph had expected the question. Knew it would come sooner rather than later.

'I haven't got any money.'

He laughed again. Got up as if to leave.

'But I do have a boat.'

He looked back.

'A boat?'

Joseph nodded. 'It's the one he'll sail out on. I'll bring it back afterwards, sail it north. It's yours.'

Joseph had thought about collateral. He had nothing else to offer. He had thought that perhaps when he said the words, he would feel something. A pang of regret. Something; but there was nothing.

'She's beautiful. Twenty-eight foot. You could make a living from her.'

He looked down at Joseph before pulling a packet of cigarettes from his jeans pocket and moving towards the door. Joseph watched him smoke through the salt-smeared window as he looked out at the industrialized sea. After a while, he blew the grey smoke away, flicked the cigarette butt, and came back in again.

He sat down, asked more questions. Asked about why this man deserved a chance. Joseph told him that he had a son, that he didn't know if he was alive, and he could see his eyes flicker to a place in his head which stored the pictures of his own son, who lived with his mother and who he barely saw. He thought, too, about the monotony of his life, the loading and unloading. The feeling that he was a facilitator, rather than an actor. That he could be replaced a thousand times over and no one would know the difference, and something within him changed. He swore under his breath, then laughed once more, nodded his head imperceptibly.

'OK,' he said, 'I'll see what I can do.'

33

Fever • Twymyn • Hima

E FA HAD HEARD HIS breath shortening over the last few days. She had woken in the night and found him hot to the touch. She opened the bedroom window and switched on a light. He was pale. She brought him some medication for his fever. Since then, his lungs had been bubbling, as if full of water. She wondered whether to call a doctor out but Emrys didn't know the new one and she didn't want to upset him.

She knew it had been too good to last. It was almost as if the last few years of withdrawing had allowed him the energy to work on the boat. Now that had been expended, there seemed to be nothing left. Efa watched over him as he slept, as dawn broke over the harbour.

She would not begrudge Nefyn or Hamza his time. Emrys had seemed happier in the last two weeks than he had been in years. Even though she knew that it was almost killing him, perhaps it was better than the way they had been living. Efa had been thinking about Nefyn and how different she seemed now. How present she was. How everything that had happened until Nefyn had invited her into the house was grainy and black and white. She was worried about her, though. Emrys's leaving was a slow one, and she had had some time to reconcile herself to it. Hamza's leaving would be sudden and in the swell of their love for each other.

It would be painful for her, Efa knew th[...]
ful remained to be seen.

Emrys was murmuring now. Efa [...]
him, placed a palm on his forehead. He [...]
sat on the edge of the bed, watching as [...]
found her form. He looked at he[...]
moment. His eyes unmoving. His mouth gaping. Trying to find the shape of words.

'Shshsh.'

'*Heb . . . hebrwng.*'

Efa looked at him. Took his hand, held it in her
lap. His wedding ring loose on his finger, the metal
worn thin.

'*Hebrwng.*'

'You're ill,' said Efa gently. 'Just a fever. You'll be
better soon.'

'The boat.'

'I know, it'll still be there.'

'*Hebrwng* Hamza . . .'

Efa looked at his face. He was determined. His
breathing heavy, heaving. Rattling. And suddenly, she
knew what he was trying to say.

'*Hebrwng?*'

He nodded.

'You want to go with Hamza?'

He nodded. Efa felt the stinging of sudden tears.
She shook her head.

'You're too ill.'

He smiled. He reached for her hand.

'No,' she said.

'I must take him.'

Efa shook her head again.

.s, please . . . Efa . . .' He was squeezing her hand
. His eyes pleading.

'Please let me go.'

This was his wish. To light the way home for
Hamza. She felt the swell of her tears in her throat. He
was saying goodbye.

Joseph had one more person to see. He was waiting for
him to finish his shift, so he walked to the lighthouse
on the headland. Sat with his back against it. Waited
for dusk. He never contemplated the sea, not like
Nefyn did. He worked it, got what he could from it,
but found no communion with it. He had naturally
lowered his gaze over the years so as not to look for the
horizon, the luminous strip that seemed to taunt him if
he accidentally caught sight of it. His father had told
him that the sea swallowed lives. That once you were
tied to it, it would take your mornings and your days,
your life and your son's life, but that somehow you
would gladly give it. He said that the sea had its own
thirst.

Tonight, though, he looked out, watched it breathing quietly, consciously. He had thought once to
emigrate. To somewhere mountainous, away from the
sea, as far as he could. He wondered if that would
make him feel at peace. Somewhere arid where dust
would stick to the back of your throat. He had shared
that dream with some girlfriends. Allowed them to
build lives in their heads. Dreams of starting again, in
mountains and forests, having children. Some girls he

had allowed to fill in all the details, before taking it all away again. But he believed it too, just for a few moments, here and there.

He wasn't sure what he wanted from the sea either. A revelation? An apology? All he knew was that he felt burdened by it. Suppressed by it. Owned by it. Its infinite expanse taunted him even tonight. It was heartless. Perhaps that was it. It gave life, sustained you and drowned you in one tide. He did not know why, but he found himself with tears on his face. For the first time in years. He felt his throat tighten and his face crumple, a wave of angry tears flood his being. He pushed them away, wiped them on his jeans as the sea breathed indifferently below.

34

Huriat albahr ◆ Môr-forwyn ◆ Mermaid

HAMZA HAD WAITED FOR hours for Emrys, but did what he could in the meantime. Once he had finished those jobs he could do alone, he turned back towards the cottage. When he told Nefyn that Emrys hadn't come, she had looked worried. There was so little left to do, but it was impossible without him. They had spent the day in relative quiet. Hamza had started writing letters in the past few days, one after the other: the events he could remember, the places he'd been held. The people who had helped him and the ones who had been cruel. A letter to his brother, to Fatima's family and to Hussein. The things he wanted to say. The goodbyes that had been denied him. He omitted where he was now, but told them simply of a friend who had been helping him. He had given Nefyn instructions to post them after he had left, in case he didn't arrive safely. A testimony of a life lived. He wrote a letter, too, for the old Doctor's wife, which Nefyn had promised to deliver. He wanted her to know how warmly her husband had spoken of her, how much she was loved. By the time he had finished, he was exhausted. He looked at the reams of paper in the blue light as if he had written a piece of fiction. So different were the events to how he was living now.

*

When Nefyn came to rest a hand on his shoulder, he pulled her towards him, and they spent the rest of the afternoon in each other's arms, waiting for the night to close around them. He wanted to feel where he was now, the letters having resurrected memories that he had to push away. Nefyn was lying beside him, holding his hands in hers, listening to him breathing, when she heard the car in the distance. She knew its sound. Her brow furrowed. She got up quietly. Moved towards the door. The light was thickening. A knock on the door. Nefyn opened it to find Efa, pale-faced and worried.

'It's Emrys,' she said, breathlessly. 'Nefyn, I need you to come.'

It was dark by the time Efa's small car drove back into the village. Most windows were curtained, lights on upstairs.

Emrys's condition had worsened throughout the day. He had been asking for Nefyn. Whispering her name as the fever burned through him. Efa knew he was too far gone for a doctor. She didn't know if Nefyn could help, but she had heard that sometimes women like her could. Nefyn had fetched her coat immediately, Hamza kissing her goodbye, both agreeing that it was safer for him to stay at the cottage.

'He's upstairs.'

Nefyn nodded. She looked small here. Out of place. Strange.

'What happened?' she asked.

'Fever. Cough. He sounds as if he's drowning.'

Nefyn took off her coat.

'Do you need anything?'

Nefyn shook her head. Efa followed her up the stairs and watched as she pushed open the door. He was lying on his side, his breathing laboured, but when he saw her, his face became illuminated, not with light but with joy. He held his breath. Smiled at her. His whole body suddenly relaxing.

'Arianell!' he said. She was so similar to her mother. Nefyn smiled. Efa moved to follow her, but Nefyn shook her head and shut the door.

Hamza tried to sleep once they had left, but he couldn't. He got up, drank coffee in the dark, reread the letters he had written, ghostly in the gloom. Efa's face had unsettled him. The fact that she had come for Nefyn a worrying testament to her husband's condition. He thought for a moment what Nefyn would do. What things she would whisper. His grandmother was from Houran and when he was ill as a child, she would be summoned with garden cress and he would be forced to drink it with honey. She would practise cupping, too, when his mother complained of a headache. Her strength, though, was in her care, her own knowledge of pain. The way her strong hands dissipated it in others. Her unwavering eyes. Knowing nods. The way she would wring out cloths in water to wash the faces of feverish children and dying relatives.

It had been warmer today; the fire remaining unlit meant it was cold now in the cottage. He watched as his breaths haunted the air. Thought of Emrys, his steady hands, his unsteady words.

His grandmother had spoken to him of a strange but beautiful woman when he was a boy, too. The same kind of wavering words as Emrys. He remembered lying in bed, watching her stitch gold geometric patterns on to the gown his grandfather would wear on a Friday. She would talk as she pierced and drew the needle over and over, turning the material under her thumb as she went. She had talked of how a young woman in an old folk tale had fallen in love with a shepherd, and how they had a beautiful daughter and lived together happily until the woman accidentally killed her lover. Hamza would listen immersed, his eyes closed, a frown forming on his forehead occasionally when his grandmother would stop to break the thread with her teeth or to re-thread the needle before continuing.

He knew not to hurry her, knew to be quiet so that he didn't interrupt the reel of her story. The woman was heartbroken and, unable to live with herself, she had left her daughter and walked into a lake, but the water would not take her. The water felt her pain, and denied her death, and changed her into a woman who could live in its depths. His grandmother had muttered that women were always punished for their strength and then denied what they wanted. She would tut, say it was a silly story and whip out his grandfather's tunic to see the progress that she had made. Each word of the stories she told him whilst trying to get him to sleep marked in a cross of gold. As Hamza grew, he had seen Atargatis's face on ancient coins.

Temples. Tourist sites. A beatific smile. Impassive. He shook his head. Got up. Walked to the living room, sat by the fireplace filled with cold ashes.

The night before, he had dreamt of drowning again. Felt the cold water slide into his lungs. The weight of the ocean on his body. He had felt the panic turn into an ecstasy of pain and then a nothingness. He had gasped himself awake, to find Nefyn fast asleep. He had sat up, forcing himself to rationalize. Pressed his palm to his chest. Felt the dull thud of his own heart-beat. He had lain down again and closed his eyes, much as he had done in the prison. He felt for every limb in turn, slowed his breathing. Thought about every sen-sation. His body was stronger now, his muscles filling his frame again. His wounds healed. His skin, even-coloured and glowing. He felt strong for the journey ahead. He lay listening to the night and Nefyn's soft breathing. He became suddenly uncomfortable in the wooden chair and moved to open the door. He walked to the bench and sat there a while.

Tonight, the dark lay heavily on him again, so that he found it difficult to breathe, pressed upon by the sea's insistence. Fatima had been buried within twenty-four hours. Only the men had attended her burial. Prayers from the Quran were said at her parents' house. Fu-nerals had changed; there would be no official period of mourning with the number of deaths so high. He had seen roadside graves, people buried where they fell. Things had changed and they had been lucky that they had been able to wash her, wrap her in a white cotton shroud, and bury her so her head was towards Mecca. They could not have asked for more under the circumstances. He had joined Fatima's family then, her father having put on a cassette of the Quran on a loop, her mother's head drooping with grief, her anxious sister holding her mother's hand. They had sat in silence, drinking bitter coffee, listening to the buzz of the words on the tape player as neighbours came to sit with them.

When he returned home, he'd collected Hussein from a neighbour. Made him some food, put him to bed. Batted away his questions for another day. In the bedroom, with Fatima's things surrounding him, he'd felt nothing, waited for a wave of grief that would not come – not yet. In place of it, a deep anger, a curious fury that burned not out of control, but with calculation, with intellect. For the sake of their son, he would not lash out, but he would do something.

For a year or two, he had tried to keep some stability in their life. Would take Hussein to his sister-in-law every day, collect him on the way home from work, but things became harder. The chaos around them increasing, the buildings crumbling. He remembered his distress mounting until it bubbled over one day when he managed to buy some fresh food, the first he had been able to source for months. Hussein looking at him quizzically. His anger growing. His students were becoming few and far between, too. Some of them caught up in narratives that perplexed him. Some of them unsure and belligerent, lost but so painfully certain as their future dissipated in front of them.

He had noticed the black car for a while, the man

he came to know waiting for him after his afternoon lectures. The careful approach they took to gauge his interest. He was flattered, of course – his expertise was well known – but now he had an avenue to help. To strike back. Their satellites, their digital mapping still not accurate enough in rough terrain. There followed meetings in cafés. And he had felt good, when they confirmed their strikes against the regime. It was only afterwards that word had reached him that they had been ambushed. And Hamza had phoned them but where once they had been communicative, they were now unreachable. Single tones of cut-off mobiles. Then, one day, they came. Bundled him into the back of a van. Hussein screaming. A neighbour running out of her house to hold him. Comfort him. He had feared that they were regime soldiers, but they were not. The shock of capture. The beating at General Reeves's hands, the colleague and close personal friend whom the General had lost in the ambush. The grudge he held. The lies they insisted that he was telling. And he had felt himself sink. Everything inaudible, far away.

The darkness was thinning now, an inky blueness seeping into the sky. The birds becoming louder. The moon thinking about dawn. He couldn't remember the last time he saw dawn break over the sea. Felt the world turn into another day on the horizon. The night lift. The heaviness dissipate. He watched as the heavens and Earth started to separate once more into distinct colours. Watched as the cold sun slid along the horizon, inhabiting, for now, the same space as the moon. Both making the world turn. Then, he heard a noise in the distance. A car, far away. A door closing. Footsteps.

She was home. She came to him, sat next to him. Leant in silently. She was cold, exhausted.

'How is he?'

She looked out to sea. The moon was fading now, the light lifting the sun.

'We'll see.'

Hamza thought of Emrys's old hands. How they knew their way instinctively around the boat. His finger-prints worn smooth now. The way his mind clung to the shape of life and the hope he could still give. Nefyn needed him; they both needed him. They sat and listened to the waves falling over each other as the tentative light grew around them.

35

Porth y Wrach ✦ *The Witch's Gate* ✦
Qaws alhajari

JOSEPH RETURNED AS DAY broke. He had hitched a ride with a lorry driver headed south. Alighted by the main road and walked into the village before first light. The landlady had given him a key and although he could have easily let himself in, he decided to walk to the cottage whilst it was still early. There were more signs of spring this morning as he kicked up golden moths walking through the long dunes. Each one fluttering then settling again as he made his way along the path. He sat outside on the bench and smoked, trying not to look too far out to sea. He flicked the ash as Nefyn came to sit beside him, carrying two cups of coffee. Joseph cleared his throat, moved his weight to the edge of the bench.

'I've been wanting to ask you something,' he said, his forehead furrowed. 'Do you remember that day on the headland?' He asked the question simply. He had been thinking a lot about it recently. How he and Nefyn had made their way to the beach alone, and how he had stumbled, slipped accidentally off the headland into the sea.

Nefyn watched him. 'Yes.'

He had panicked. He couldn't find a foothold and the waves were butting him up against the wall of the cliff. He had started swallowing water. Screaming. And she had stood there, looking down at him.

'Why didn't you shout? Why didn't you help me?'

He had had nightmares about it for years. The look on her face. Her strength in the water, his weakness. The sea saturating his clothes, his hair, making him heavy. His arms numb and weakening. And he had held that memory close to his heart. The way she had looked at him, impassive, immobile, as if she were waiting for something. And then their father had come running, jumped in. An arm under his chin. The feeling of being thrown on to hard ground. The admonishments for being so stupid. Their mother had washed him, put him to bed, whilst Nefyn watched silently.

'Why didn't you help me, Nefyn?' He couldn't look at her even now.

'Because I knew you could swim,' she said.

'No, I couldn't.'

'Yes, you could. You were just scared to.'

Joseph took this in.

'If you had been scared enough, you would have swum, known that you could do it. Grown into yourself.'

Joseph flicked his cigarette.

'And I knew that if I saved you, you'd hate me for it. Every day.' The gulls were calling now, each one looking for today's offerings on the tideline. 'The next time, when you were jumping into the sea at Porth y Wrach, with your friends—'

'I was fine.'

Nefyn shook her head.

'No, you were going to fall that day . . . I felt it. I knew it. I came because you needed me, but then you were *so* angry.' Joseph was quiet. The thought that she may not have known how to treat *him* strange. He nodded. They sat in silence a moment.

'It's going to have to be Saturday morning, then,' he said eventually, still not looking at her.

'That's three days,' Nefyn answered.

'There'll be less people, on the boats and at the lookouts. Things will go easier.' Nefyn thought about this as Joseph continued. 'There's a smaller freight ship going to the South of France. There'll be some papers for him on the boat. He'll have to make his own way from there. If we miss the highest tide, it means another week's wait, and we can't risk that.'

Nefyn could hear Hamza in the house, walking around, washing, dressing. His sounds had become part of the place.

'I'll bring the boat out of the boatshed the night before. Moor it on the rocks. There's no other way without drawing a crowd.'

Hamza came outside. Sat with them a moment.

'Emrys is ill,' said Nefyn. 'I went to him last night.'

Joseph turned to look at her.

'You went there?'

Nefyn nodded.

'He wants to take Hamza out.'

Joseph shook his head.

'He's too old.'

'Please, Joseph.'

'You'll be putting his life in his hands,' he said gesturing to Hamza. 'His mind's not right, we only have one chance, and if he's ill as well . . . We need him as a decoy, to draw some attention away from what we're doing.'

Nefyn let the subject rest, knew there was no point pushing him.

'How far is the boat from finished?'

Hamza shrugged his shoulders.

'Not far.'

Joseph nodded.

'We'd better have a look, then,' he said. Joseph got up, glad of the excuse to do so. He waited for Hamza to get a coat, then he turned and led the way to the cove, leaving Nefyn looking out to sea.

The Lieutenant Colonel's wife had been waiting for him when he got home the night before. He hadn't yet told her; one of the other army wives had done him that particular courtesy. A tense exchange had ensued. She couldn't do it any more. She wanted to be able to put down roots. Make a home. She wanted to talk. He stood stiffly. Forty years of training, of learning always to be dispassionate, were difficult to shrug off. He had pointed out to her how things could be smoothed over. Asked her to lower her voice. Stop embarrassing him. The walls were paper-thin. Long silences. Scrappy words. He had told her that this was the best opportunity of his career. This was their ticket away from here, all she had to do was hang on. Hang on? Hang on was all she ever did. Hang around. Hang on. Hang on to what? The strictures and structures that had provided a scaffold for their lives were now squeezing her. Constricting the life from her. The straight lines of promotion hemming them in. And then she had quietened, her rounded shoulders and concave chest and ache for a life she had not lived. She had talked herself into silence. Heavy, damp and muted. Swollen-faced and still. He had asked her to give him a few days to sort this mess out and had resolved to take some, any kind of action.

The Lieutenant Colonel's movements had been severely restricted. Not through regulations but through his own irritation and embarrassment. It was a small barracks and everyone would be speculating. Seeing the temporarily promoted Captain was a particular source of irritation. He stayed in his quarters and read the report over and over again. It was his dealing with the soldier that he was under investigation for. There was very little he could do to excuse the file he had faked, though he could say that it had been necessary for covering up the story about Prisoner B, and he was sure that the General would back him on that. But he was determined to disprove any connection to the soldier's death. The soldier's property had been confiscated and nothing of note was found there. No personal letters, and crucially, no indication that he was suffering from a mental illness. He wasn't particularly liked, it transpired, but no one had a reason to hurt him.

He began by pulling all the records he had of the Captain's history and throwing them on to his desk, then he sat combing them for any indiscretion that might be useful, and then he reread the report of the drowned soldier. When he finished, he pushed himself away from his desk, got up and looked for his coat. He needed to see the cove, where they said the soldier had entered the water. The police had said that there was a cottage overlooking it, and that they had found a brother and sister living there, but nothing out of the ordinary. He made his way across the barracks, keeping his head down, trying not to draw attention. He was in his civilian clothes, and knew that some soldiers would enjoy it; the fact that they did not have to officially acknowledge him. He didn't mind that; it was those who looked at him with compassion that he found most humiliating, as if he was suddenly vulnerable, someone to be pitied.

He crossed out of the barracks and took the path that he had followed all those years ago, when he had first come to the site. It was beginning to get dark so he walked at some pace, tasting the salt in the air. He could feel his body warming, his legs stretching after days of confinement. He had missed the trekking, if truth be told. The yomps. The feeling of exhausting himself to the point of oblivion. The piles of paperwork had replaced the job.

He could hear the sea as he came nearer. He traced the coast with his eyes, looked for where it dipped inwards to the south. He quickened, the darkness keeping pace with him, until he saw it, the cottage in the distance, perching precariously on the edge of the cliff. He stopped, blew out his chest. Some colour on his face. He breathed deeply for a moment before moving closer and closer through the couch grass and the reeds, until he was outside the cottage. It was quiet. No sounds except the sound of the sea in the cove. He looked over, walked slowly towards the cliff edge. As he peered down into the cove, he heard a noise behind him and he turned to see a young woman. Dark-haired and still. He was breathless.

'I'm sorry, you live here?'

Nefyn nodded. Noticed that, despite the civilian clothes, he had army boots on his feet. His regulation haircut. He walked towards her.

'Yes,' she said cautiously.

He nodded, the breeze catching his hair. 'I suppose it's quiet.' He found himself struggling for words, his resolve dissipating under her gaze. 'I'm sorry, I just wanted to see . . .' He shook his head. 'I don't know what I wanted to see.'

Down in the boatshed, Joseph placed a hand on Hamza's arm. Gestured upwards to the cliff-top. Hamza stopped working as the light breeze carried voices their way. They had finished the boat. She was ready, but they had to repair the trailer that would carry her down the beach. The man turned.

'I'll just go down,' the Lieutenant Colonel said. 'You don't mind, do you?'

'I wouldn't if I were you.' He looked back at her uncertainly. 'It's too dark. The path's too steep. You won't get back up before the tide comes in.'

The Lieutenant Colonel looked out to sea. Even though he had lived here for years, he relied on data to tell him about the tides. He had thought that maybe it would become second nature to him, but it hadn't. He looked out again. Couldn't be sure. Nefyn smiled.

'It's dangerous, that's all.'

The Lieutenant Colonel nodded.

'You haven't seen any strangers around, have you?'

Nefyn tilted her head. He found her unnerving. Her stillness.

'I mean, someone you don't know?'

Nefyn smiled softly again.

'Only you.'

The Lieutenant Colonel laughed.

'Of course. I'm sorry to have disturbed you. I really don't know what I was thinking.'

Agitated, he couldn't bring himself to leave just yet. Peered into the cottage, saw the fireplace in the gloom. The chair. A compass on a small table. 'Have you always lived here?' His question seemed sincere. Nefyn nodded. He laughed, shook his head, trying to order his thoughts. 'Perhaps she's right . . .' he said. Nefyn waited. 'My wife, she was saying that she'd like to stay in one place for some time, see what it's like.'

Nefyn thought he suddenly looked a lot older, the colour in his cheeks gone.

'We've always moved, moved and moved so we don't really . . .' His voice fractured. 'It's the great lie, isn't it? The race to the top, when there isn't one really.' He smiled sadly. 'I'm so sorry,' he apologized.

Nefyn looked at him steadily. His face unsure. Lost.

'I'm so sorry.'

Then, he started walking away. Nefyn turned. Watched him go. His shoulders curved now. Soft. His head looking downwards. She watched his figure grow smaller and smaller before he disappeared into the dunes. She turned back to the cottage, and her eyes alighted on Hamza's compass on the table by the fire.

36

Hebrwng ♦ Escort ♦ Murafaq

AFTER NEFYN LEFT, EFA had continued to nurse Emrys. When she had gone to him, his eyes had seemed clearer. His voice stronger. He had held her hand tightly, pulled her near. She had lain then by his side, until he had whispered his thanks for all the things she had done for him. She had asked Mary to come and sit with him now, and walked the coast path towards the church. She did not know why she had come, but something about the coolness of that interior had lured her. She pushed the door open, and rather than reach for the broom as she usually would, she left the sand that had blown in, preferring to listen instead to the sound of the sea breathing against the church walls.

We always want more, that's what the old Doctor had told her. However blessed and happy our lives have been, however thankful we know we should feel, we always want more. She had seen it in the Doctor's widow's face as she fell into the arms of her sons. The sudden loneliness. The going home without him.

When she was younger, Efa had thought that time would prepare her, that the years would wear away the fear that she felt, but they hadn't, of course. He was all she had known. The first man she had been with. They had moved through the years from young lovers to friends and back to lovers again, as most couples did.

She had watched him age, watched his cheeks redden with veins, his skin wear thin. The softening of his face and his smile. And he had witnessed her thickening waist, her stubborn hair, the lumpy veins of her legs. He had placed a hand on her waist in the dead of night when they had gone to bed in silence after an argument. A gentle reminder that they shouldn't fight. He had been the one who sat with her in the hospital waiting room when the baby they had lost wouldn't come away. He was the one who had taken her to the café afterwards, and talked to her about the caravan holiday he had booked and how he wanted to buy her a new flask, bringing a gentle smile to her face though it was ruddy and blotchy with crying. And it was with him that she had laughed and talked of getting old as they danced barefoot along the harbour wall when they were young, and it was with him that she had talked about being young when in old age they had looked out at the same wall, with the dark sea breathing beyond.

She heard the bare feet on the tiles and knew instinctively it was Nefyn. She came to sit beside her in the pew. Laid her head on her shoulder.

'I knew you were here,' she whispered.

Efa nodded silently. Her vision blurring.

'I'm looking for strength,' she said simply.

'He'll have a safe passage,' said Nefyn.

Efa felt her body relax. She swallowed down her tears.

'He's a little better today.'

Nefyn knew that already.

'I know.'

Efa looked at her hands. Nefyn placed hers over them. Efa didn't know whether or not to pray.

'I wish I had listened to myself earlier,' Nefyn said. 'I wish I had opened the door years ago.'

Efa smiled. Felt Nefyn's hair on her cheek.

'I wish you had, too.'

They sat in silence for a moment, Efa struggling with the burning of tears in her throat.

'I wanted you to know something about my mother.' Efa listened, Nefyn's voice seamless and smooth. 'I think she'd like you to know.' Nefyn's skin was startlingly white and soft against her own. She opened her hand, held Nefyn's palm on hers. Tried to memorize the picture it made. 'She left us. She went back to the sea.'

Efa nodded.

'I was scared about your father . . . that maybe he'd done something . . .'

Nefyn shook her head.

'No.'

Nefyn smoothed out Efa's skin in her fingers.

'She wanted to go. But . . .'

Efa listened as Nefyn's voice became even softer, delicate, nebulous almost.

'She sent a storm for him.' Efa's eyes turned. Nefyn continued. 'She waited until we were old enough to be without him.'

Efa had often wondered about the ferocity of the storm that took Nefyn's father. Such an experienced sailor would never have ventured forth in such conditions.

'That storm that came from nowhere?' Efa asked. Nefyn nodded.

'It was for him. For taking her, for forcing her to have children, for beating her . . .' Nefyn quietened. 'I watched her go.' Her eyes were far away now. 'My father thought it was sudden, but it wasn't. It took months.' She smiled sadly. 'The quietness, the walks she took in the night, the praying.' Efa thought of Arianell in the church. 'It was killing her. I could see it. And then, she waited until my father was fishing, sent Joseph on an errand.' Efa listened, the silence around them pressing on each word. 'It was like she'd found something . . . she always said it was a cloak, but it was something more than that. She wasn't handed her freedom, she took it. She had no choice. It was life or death.'

Efa thought of Nefyn's father. The boy she had known in school. The way he had grown. The way Efa had felt when his body had been found. The nothingness.

'I think it was harder for Joseph to understand.'

Efa thought about leaving a child. Thought of the desperation that that would take.

'Anyway,' said Nefyn quietly, 'I think she would have liked you to know.'

Efa turned to her.

'And what about you?' Efa asked, still holding her hand. 'The storm that brought you Hamza?' Efa paused for a moment. 'Did she send that, too?'

Nefyn shrugged.

'Perhaps.'

Efa let her head tilt against Nefyn's and they sat

together, the tableau of the Crucifixion on the stained-glass window glowing above them.

～

Hamza was always restless before a journey. It was as if he left days before he departed. When Hussein was small and work used to take him away, he would be absent in his head long before his departure, and too present physically, hugging Hussein until it irritated him, and arguing with Fatima. Part of preparing for any journey involved the possibility of not coming back.

He had borrowed a bag from Joseph, packed some clothes and some food. He had the sextant and the maps, which he had tried to memorize. He had the old phone too, given to him by Joseph with strict instructions not to turn it on until they were way out of The Range. He had filled it with a list of numbers from Joseph's contacts.

When Nefyn came back from the church, she found him walking the floor agitatedly. She closed the door quietly behind her, watched him a moment.

'What if he's dead? What if Hussein is dead? When I didn't know, I could . . . I could hope. I don't know what to do if . . .' His voice faded away. Nefyn stood, her back to the door.

'What if he's alive?' she countered. 'What if he's waiting for you?' There was a fear in his eyes that Nefyn had not seen before.

'I don't know what I'm going back to.'

He stopped walking. Surrendered. He moved

towards her and they held each other quietly. Then he leant her backwards, looked at her closely.

'Why won't you come?' He was searching her face now. 'You could come with me.'

Nefyn shook her head.

'I've told you.'

'You said you can't come, that's all.'

'I can't leave here, Hamza.'

'Why?'

'Because I can't.' Nefyn shook her head. 'I'm sorry, I . . .'

'Please. Tell me why. Help me understand.'

Nefyn tried to find the words.

'I've told you, we could go and find Hussein, we could find a place for the two of us by the sea.'

Nefyn had tears in her eyes. She shook her head again. 'No.'

'You can't love me . . . not like I love you.' He let her go. His anger souring. He studied her. 'You're scared. But you don't belong here, Nefyn. Not like this. You could come, you could be free. Free of all of this. This thing you hide behind.' He was angry again now. His eyes flitting. 'What I found here, what we have . . . you can't throw it away!'

'Stop it.'

'Is it so cheap to you? What we have?' Nefyn's face grew paler. 'Or are you not brave enough?'

'I am brave enough.'

'Then come with me.'

Nefyn's anger flared with an unexpected heat.

'I said NO!'

He could tell she was wounded, became aware

of her breathing. She was pulling away from him again.

'They're looking for you; you have to go as soon as possible,' she said evenly.

'Who's looking for me?'

'A man came here, when you were with the boat. You have to go. You have no choice. They're closing in.' Then she turned. Opened the door, walked out. Hamza thought of following her, but decided against it. He picked up a cup from the table and threw it against the wall.

Outside, Nefyn heard the smashing of ceramic. She tried to block it out as she walked. He was angry. She knew that. He was lashing out. She knew that too, but it hurt. It hurt, and the two days they had left were so brief already. She walked to Porth y Wrach, to the edge of the cliff, and without looking around, she slid down the cliff-top, and into the water. She let herself drop like a stone to the bottom of the sea. And she sat there, her eyes darkening in the grey water, her back to the cliff wall.

37

Launch • 'iitlaq alqarib • Bwrw'r cwch i'r dŵr

JOSEPH OPENED THE BOATSHED in the cool morning air.
He had borrowed a small fishing boat for a few
days, moored her out in the cove and brought a dinghy
to land. He looked at his father's boat. He had not
sailed in her since he was sixteen, since she was brought
home. The tide was rising, he could hear it, the sea lap-
ping rather than drawing. He looked up at the cliff
edges, knowing he would have to be as discreet as
practicality would allow. Many hands had helped her
up the shallow beach into the shed, but it would just be
him trying to launch her out. She was on a trailer, but
he would have to find a way of winching her to sea, at
least past the tideline. Anchor her there so she would
be let down and buoyed once again by the tide.

He kicked the trailer chocks, picked up the hitch.
Felt her weight balanced in his hand. He pulled and
felt her move towards him, her weight bearing down
on him. This would usually require the help of two to
three men. He started to move backwards as she sprang
towards him. There was an incline to the ramp into
the boatshed and she ran with it, her weight increasing
with every step. He braced himself against her, breathing hard, tried to stop her overwhelming him, knocking
him over. Backwards he inched, until her bows edged
out of the boatshed for the first time in ten years. Her
shape distinct. Feminine. He gasped as the tyres hit the

sand, her weight deadening. He had thought this might happen. The cove had changed imperceptibly over time, its depth, the way the sand was distributed. It was not the same cove as it had been when the boat had been dragged up the beach. It was deeper, the tideline different. She was stuck. He pulled, his body warming, sweat on his back. He swore, spat, tugged his jumper roughly over his head and threw it down. He went to find some rocks. As heavy as he could carry, he placed them carefully in the stern of the boat to raise her back a little, take the pressure off the hitch. He carried them, one after another, until he felt a shift in her weight. He yanked at the handle of the trolley again and she moved a few inches. Heartened, he tried again, leaning all his weight backwards, and he started to pull the boat, inch by inch, towards the sea.

The Lieutenant Colonel lay in the room he kept in the officers' quarters, his head heavy after another sleepless night. He had come back to the barracks, opened a bottle of whiskey. Hadn't returned the call from his wife. He got up, rubbed his head, swung his legs unsteadily to the floor. He needed to shave.

The investigations team had arrived but the protocol was so painfully slow. He knew this, had been grateful for it in the past, but now he needed them to conclude their investigation, needed to escape this awful limbo. He listened as exercises were conducted in the yard outside. He moved to the bathroom, splashed his face with water.

He had dreamt, too. Vivid, lucid dreams. He had seen the young woman in the cove. There was something about her that he could not put his finger on. It wasn't an attraction on his part, it wasn't that, but she had been interesting. Her calmness. Her eyes. Something about her that was repellent but also magnetic. He didn't know why he hadn't walked down into the cove. He had trusted her. Taken her word, and as an officer that was something he would never usually do. You couldn't be advised by others unquestioningly, it went against the very nature of what he was trained to do. He thought it odd – perhaps that was it – that he had complied so willingly with her suggestion.

He ran his fingers over his stubble and reached for the soap. As he lathered his face, he thought of how the UADs were being shipped to Portsmouth. How it was being done on a Saturday. It would draw less attention, but they were loaded and ready. As he scraped the blade down his jawline, he thought too of how the Captain would profit from this success, and as he did so, the tension in his hand made it falter, nicking a cut on his face. He swore and pulled the skin tighter, tried to ignore the blood leaking into the white lather. He couldn't let that happen. He'd worked too hard. Something other than suicide had happened to that soldier, he was sure of it, and when he found out what it was, he would be reinstated, the fact of the forged paperwork forgiven under the circumstances. The Captain put back in his place.

He finished shaving, dabbed the cut with a little aftershave. Felt it sting. He looked better now. His head clearing. He thought once more about the girl, and her cottage, the dark fireplace and the books and the compass on a chain, lying on the small table. And then he stopped, froze. Every muscle in his body tense. Without pulling on a shirt, he ran in his vest towards the barracks offices, swearing under his breath as he went. He barged into the building but was stopped by a guard. He tried to push past him and when he was pushed back, he looked at him in confusion. He wasn't an acting officer now. He had no access. The Lieutenant Colonel started shouting at him, and more soldiers arrived. It was only when the Captain appeared that he started shouting about the compass, about how he knew that Prisoner B was alive and that he was at the cottage by the cove. The Captain looked at the two men holding the Lieutenant Colonel back, and nodded at them to take him to the guardroom so that he could calm down. The Lieutenant Colonel started swearing. Fighting. They didn't know what they were talking about. The Captain watched him being dragged away. His arms flailing, blood on his face, the smell of whiskey on his breath.

38

Axis ♦ Mihwar ♦ Echel

THE PERIGEAN TIDE CAME only three or four times a year. The moon would leave its apogee and bow to take a closer look at Earth. When this coincided with a spring tide, the cove would be at its fullest. On these windless nights, the water was black, deep, still. The perigean tide was glass-like, its surface reflective so that you could see its constellations on the water.

Hamza had waited for Nefyn to come home, and when she had, he had held her and cried. She had wiped his tears, waited for them to subside, his sorrow seeping into her. Then, she had led him, her clothes still soaking, to the cove, the walk down much shorter than usual as the waterline rose to the door of the boat-shed. The boatshed door was now gaping, empty, the vessel waiting on the smooth water in the bay.

She had taken off her cardigan, yanked it from her shoulders, pulled at his jumper, and led him to the water. It felt strange. Not cold. Not warm. It was the temperature of blood, almost impalpable. Like light. It was like swimming in air. He froze as the water threatened to engulf him and she could sense his hesitancy. He had not been in the sea since that night. The Doctor's face disappearing into the darkness. The sound of metal bending, glass shattering. He could almost feel the violence of that night in the water, but Nefyn kissed his hand softly and pulled him into the darkness.

The blackness rose up around them, the moon pressing over the cottage above. The cliffs monumental from here. They rounded the boat, watched as she rocked with their movements. The boat was sound, quiet, beautiful. She breathed with each ripple as if glad to be back in the water. Nefyn smiled at Hamza and gestured for him to follow her. He watched as she swam, her skin glowing whiter in the water, her hair darkening in strands around her face. Moving here was nothing to her. Effortless. He followed her, trusting, like a child, further and further out. And when she was happy, she asked him to lie on his back. She swam beside him, holding his head. Pressed her face to the side of his face.

'Look up,' she whispered.

He relaxed. Thought of his father once more.

Don't fight it, his voice in his head. And this time, there was no panic. No grappling, no fighting for air. He tilted his head backwards, the pupils of his eyes widening. And there he saw the stars, fierce and vital in the night sky. Each one vibrant. Patterns upon patterns. Constellations. Signs. Symbols. Words, perhaps. He gasped. They were all around them too, not just above, they were wherever he looked, at the apex of the world and at the horizon.

'It's Fatima's globe,' she said quietly. Hamza smiled. 'Trust,' she whispered again, kissing the side of his face. The blackness of the night enfolded them, and blurred the separation of water and air so that they hung between two worlds, the Earth turning around them.

The Lieutenant Colonel sat on the lower bunk, head in hands. His fury and shame a storm inside him. He would get up every now and again and kick the walls in frustration. The guard outside would relay this information to the Captain and he, in turn, would tell the guard to keep him there a while longer for him to cool down. The Captain had taken a lengthy call from General Reeves that morning. He'd explained to him that he had no idea why the Lieutenant Colonel would falsify a soldier's records like that. They'd discovered, too, after talking a little longer, that the Captain's father had attended the same college as the General. The Captain had assured him that Prisoner B was gone, so that business was concluded, and since the Lieutenant Colonel was to be removed for causing the death of Owens by a campaign of bullying, they could draw a line under everything and look to the future. General Reeves had told him that he thought he had a very glittering future indeed. After he'd put down the phone, the Captain listened to the Lieutenant Colonel shouting and raging in the guardroom and considered again what he had said about Prisoner B and that cove. There might be something in it, he thought, but the UADs were being dispatched early the next morning so it would have to wait.

39

Ffarwelio ✦ Farewell ✦ Tawdie

EFA BAKED EMRYS HIS favourite cake, packed it into a box for him. He spent the day sitting at the window looking out at the harbour. She washed his clothes, too, put some spare ones in his bag and fetched his old sailing gear, his boots and waterproof coat from the cupboard under the stairs. She pressed them to her as she put them to air; they still smelled of oil and boats and the sea.

She had knitted him a jumper, to an old pattern. A type of gansey with the shapes of waves and fish in its weave. She had pulled it over his head for him to try it on, and he wouldn't take it off after that. There was nothing more then that she could do but sit with him and hold his hand, looking out at the harbour. They had an early start in the morning. Joseph wanted them at the cove at four thirty, and Nefyn had suggested that they might like to stay at the cottage, but Efa had declined. She had wanted him home. For their last night.

She had thought of the things that she would miss, and what she had decided she would miss most was the drinking of tea in contented silence. The sound of him moving about. That was all. After all these years, but they seemed like the most important things now. She made them some supper which they took in the living room, and carried tea to him. He had tried to get a slice of the cake out of her too, but she had resisted. It was one of their games, her trying to keep cake from him before it had even cooled down properly.

Then, when the colourful lights around the harbour had been illuminated, they had placed his bag by the door, and walked upstairs. He had insisted on sleeping in his fisherman's jumper, and she had no strength left to argue with him. It might be difficult to get him ready anyway so early, so at least if he were dressed it would be something. She held him to her, felt him rub her fingers between his, and when he felt her cry into his back, he found a sudden strength.

'It's all right, my darling,' he said. 'It's all right.'

❦

Joseph had come to stay at the cottage and wasn't there for long before he realized it wasn't his home any more. His things were still there, of course, his clothes, but they had been inhabited by someone else. Perhaps he had changed, too.

The three of them ate together, and then Joseph and Hamza smoked a while, Joseph smiling as the older man coughed, having not smoked for so long. Then he went for a walk, so Hamza and Nefyn could be by themselves. His body was aching already from the monumental task of getting the boat into the water. It was a relief to stretch his legs, his arms. He had walked as far as Porth y Wrach, looked down at the spot where he almost drowned all those years ago, and thought about what Nefyn had said. He had been defined by her, it was true, but he had also let himself be defined by his fear. He thought for a moment of his father. The way he had blamed his mother for things. He felt a discomfort in the pit of his stomach.

He had watched Hamza and Nefyn, too. The way they were at one, almost, and he had felt something akin to jealousy. That closeness he had observed in others that he seemed incapable of. He wondered about the relief that that would bring. The sense of belonging. He looked up at the sky. The full tide. Thought of all that he had to do tomorrow. He had been reluctant to let Emrys go with Hamza, but the old man had persuaded him that it was his duty and that Joseph, being younger and stronger, would be a better decoy. He looked across at the army base in the distance, bristling and black. He knew they had eyes everywhere. Watchtowers. What they were attempting to do felt ridiculous. It required a miracle, but everyone he had talked to seemed to want one. To believe it could be done. And slowly but surely, Joseph had almost come to believe it too.

Nefyn and Hamza lay in each other's arms. Their words gone. There was nothing more to be said. They had held and gazed upon each other, each trying to etch the other on their memory. An act of remembrance in the present. She tried to secure the tone of his eyes in her mind, he tried to etch the angles of her body into his, and together they made a map. Of someone they had known. Somewhere they had inhabited. A point of reference that would be a fixed mark upon the world. Unmoving. Rooted. They marked on it the thoughts they had had together, the visions, the depth of their feelings. The longitude and latitude of their wonder. Then, when they had finished, they slept. Soundly and deeply, for they would need all their strength for tomorrow.

Tide ✦ *Llanw* ✦ *Almadu*

THE COVE HAD ALWAYS called things to it. Her father would blame the jutting headland, saying that it slowed the tide so that it brought forth its offerings. Her mother used to say that it was something much more than that. That the sea would show you what you needed it to, in its own time, and that the only thing you could do was wait.

Nefyn turned to see Joseph leading Emrys down the cove path, gently, patiently. Hamza helping Efa behind him. It was not dawn yet, the dark water moving slowly in the gloom. The strandline was high today, the objects brought in by the tide close under the cliff. Nefyn stood on the sea's edge as Joseph brought Emrys to stand by her. Efa followed on Hamza's arm, her knuckles white, her hands tense. Their breath billowing in the morning air.

Nefyn then watched as Efa tidied Emrys's collar. She handed him his bag. He kissed her as he had done a thousand times before when he went to sea, but this time, Efa's hands were shaking. Emrys nodded to Joseph, who walked him into the sea, out to the boat, helped him in. The water noisy in its agitation. Joseph watched as he found his feet on board, his eyes already looking for things to do, instinct taking over. Joseph waded back towards them. He nodded at Hamza.

Nefyn looked up at him, and smiled softly. She

walked with him into the water, until it was up to her shoulders, and she watched as he pulled himself into the boat. He knelt back down, leant over the side to kiss her. Then, he slipped the chain and compass over his head and slid it on to her neck. He kissed her face, her closed eyes. The tears on her cheeks.

'Trust,' she said.

Hamza nodded silently, his voice choked.

'Nothing is impossible,' he whispered, holding her face.

Emrys had started the engine, the swell beginning to rock the boat. They pressed their foreheads together once more, held hands, until the force of the water parted them. Nefyn stood there as the boat pulled away, Emrys sailing and Hamza looking backwards. Just then, she felt an arm around her. It was Joseph, pulling her towards him. Looking outwards. On the shore behind them was Efa, her shoulders high, pale-faced in the dawn light.

Joseph knew what he had to do. They had talked about it, over and over. They would wait, wait until Emrys and Hamza had gained a head start before Joseph would take the borrowed boat and sail right into The Range. This should draw enough attention to warrant them coming to investigate, giving the others a chance to clear The Range on the path unseen.

Joseph and Nefyn waded back to shore, listening as the sound of the boat's engine was swallowed up by the expanse of the sea. The other boat was moored near by. Joseph looked at his watch. He would give them forty minutes, and then he would have to move.

*

On the boat, Emrys worked silently. He knew the points of the bay, looked back in reference at the coast. The sea was quiet, still.

'Emrys? Please, give me some work.' Emrys nodded. Hamza got up, knowing that what they were doing was ridiculous. The meeting of two vessels in alignment on the vast water, and now that he looked out he could see its expanse. It opened up as they sailed on, the sound of the waves settling around them in the open ocean. They were part of it now. Its fabric. At its mercy and humour. They sailed on, on the invisible path that Joseph had given them, bound for the endless sea.

4 I

Gweddi • Prayer • Duea'

JOSEPH TOOK HIS LEAVE and ran up the path to the cliffs. He would go to his boat and wait. He gestured to Efa to look after Nefyn. She was shivering, her clothes wet, her arms down by her sides as if not noticing the cold. Efa placed her arm around her as they stood on the beach unable to move somehow. Wanting to bear witness. Nefyn's face framed by her wet hair, her eyes drawn to the horizon. Efa tried to rub Nefyn's arms, warm her up as they stood, their eyes searching for signs of the vanished boat. Efa could feel her getting colder so she took off her coat, placed it around her shoulders. Nefyn glanced towards her for a moment, her eyes seemingly not recognizing her.

'Nefyn?'

Nefyn smiled, started whispering. Her eyes drawn back to the sea. She had not felt the strength of her abilities. Not fully. But she felt them now. Something rising in her. Her mother had warned her when she was a child that this, allowing herself to feel – it strengthened her. The words came from somewhere she didn't know. Efa listened to her. Language rising through her. A memory.

'*Kyd karui vi morfa cassaa vi don, Digoneis don dries oer kleis y ron.*' Something she had carried with her perhaps from nursery rhymes and songs. Over and over her blue lips recited. Efa kept hold of her, felt her quivering in her arms.

It was the wind that changed first. A strange insistence. A wailing. And it had risen quickly. A squall, tugging at Efa's dress. The sea darkening suddenly. Efa could feel it. In the air around her. In Nefyn. In the sound of the sea. She looked up, worried, but the small boat had disappeared from sight.

'*Kyd karui vi morfa cassaa vi don, Digoneis don dries oer kleis y ron.*'

The Captain had seen off the consignment of Unmanned Aerial Drones and returned to his quarters. Looked out of the window and saw the darkening sky. He frowned, wondered why he hadn't been warned of any change in the weather pattern. He looked at his watch. Thought once again of the Lieutenant Colonel, and picked up the phone.

'Yes, it's probably worth taking a look . . . Yes . . . Send two men, that should be fine . . .' He put the phone down. It wouldn't do any harm to check, and if they did pick up a lead, then it would have been on his watch and would reflect well on him.

Joseph pushed the boat to water and jumped in. He was ready. He had made sure he had a faster boat. It gave him a fighting chance at least of keeping them at bay for a little while. He heard the engine pull as he chugged out of the harbour. He motored directly for The Range in the exact opposite direction to where Hamza and Emrys would be by now. They would surely pick him up. Fire a warning shot. Come out with boats. It was difficult to know. He hadn't heard them testing at night for a while, so he wasn't too concerned about the missiles; it was more about what they would do when he refused to leave The Range.

The soldiers approached the cottage in a Land Rover. They knocked on the door, and on receiving no answer, let themselves in. They had been given permission to enter by their commanding officer if no one was there. It was a case of national security, after all. They looked around, one of them tall enough to have to bow his head. They took in the small fireplace. The small rooms. Oppressive. Still. There was nothing they could see. They began opening drawers. Upending books. They searched with a ruthless efficiency, scattering objects as they went. Violating. Invading. Taking apart. It was not long until they found the letters. With foreign addresses, some of them in Syria. One soldier looked to the other, went to call the base on his radio, was ordered to bring the letters back immediately.

42

Watchtower ♦ *Y tûr* ♦ *Burj almuraqaba*

THE GUARDS AT THE watchtower were immediately alerted and picked up a vessel in The Range. They scrambled the army boats and requested helicopter backup. By the time the soldiers had climbed down the ladders to their boats, the sea was heaving. The wind had picked up exponentially, skimming foam from the top of every wave. It had come from nowhere, this storm, ill-tempered and violent. They radioed back to the command tower to see whether they should proceed. They were given the affirmative.

Joseph sailed across The Range just as he had done as a child. Freely. With no restriction. Like he had done before the army had sectioned and separated the sea, before they had created boxes in his mind. He felt the storm mewling at first before it strengthened around him. Its intensity palpable. He felt it seep into his consciousness. His fear growing. It didn't matter how many years he'd been at sea, it was instinct. The noise of the water as it raged shot fear through the hardest of men. The winds were cross-cutting the water angrily, without order or pattern, knocking Joseph repeatedly off his feet. Then, a flare. He looked up to see a blinding red light above him. A swooshing past. Another. Warnings. He knew then that they had seen him. He began to sicken to his stomach, his back knocking against the stern, the foamy spray on his front. He scanned the horizon, waiting for the military boat to come into view.

Emrys's mind had been occupied as they sailed from the bay. Time had stood still for him as he moved backwards in his mind to all those years when he had been at one with a boat. Her invisible course. He had remembered the thrill of riding a wave, of carving a path that no one else could see, of being a part of something so much bigger. He felt all this as the waves grew up around them, and he and Hamza sailed at the edge of the squall. Then, as they entered the storm proper, the waves butted and broke, becoming more violent. The movement of the boat knocking him from his feet. His attempts at getting up becoming fewer and fewer. His adrenaline dropped, his resolve weakened. He was soaked through, his fragile strength almost spent.

Hamza had taken over, but his scant knowledge failed him. He fought the sea. Felt the full force of the squall on his face. The waves had become bigger, taller, each one raising the boat, before letting it plummet downwards. Spray coming in on both sides. He saw the fear in Emrys's eyes as he sat in the bottom of the boat, his head knocking against its side. Blood in his hair. And then, as Hamza's arms burned against the tiller, something happened. He felt a great stillness around him. He let go. He stopped fighting. He thought of what Nefyn had said to him. He pulled his hand away and stood. The sea tossing the little boat as if it were nothing. Then, he moved on his hands and knees across the boat and sat down with Emrys. Put his arm around him, centring his thoughts on Hussein. The old man closed his eyes, his heart rising, thinking of Efa when she was young, the softness of her eyes; felt the warmth of Hamza's arm around him, the world moving beneath them. Their laughable smallness. His shoulders relaxed as he felt a wonder grow inside him and they both sat trusting in the boat, each leaving his fate to his own god.

The watchmen in the tower along the coast had been talking. There were rumours about the Lieutenant Colonel, that he'd lost his mind. They had been discussing this when they caught the tail end of an object on their radar. There were sometimes anomalies. Things they couldn't explain, and they had thought that maybe this was one of those times. They knew the boats had been scrambled to an incident at The Range and they knew the helicopter was on its way.

The noise was deafening. The helicopter was lurching in the sky overhead. Joseph clung on to the side of the boat, his legs stretched out to brace his body. He was exhausted. He had put up his hood, in order to cover his face, to buy some more time. The army boat had turned back. There was a great, metallic din. A voice overhead. Telling him to leave The Range, that he was in military waters. He was asked to put his hands up. He resisted. He was warned again. His heart clenching and unclenching. They asked him to show his face but he could hardly hear. They would usually have sent down a soldier, commandeered the boat, but it was too rough for that. They warned him to turn back. Joseph looked at his watch. He needed more time. He steadied himself. Pushed himself back on the floor, his mind still on the beach with Nefyn.

Her eyes were closed now, her breathing laboured. Efa knelt behind her, tried to prop her up on the sand, but she was so cold. So cold to the touch.

'Nefyn . . . please. Stop.' Efa was trying to reach her but she was fading. Whispering. Her words like water, unceasing. Flowing. Urging the storm on. Efa could feel it weakening her. In front of her eyes.

'Nefyn, please.'

Joseph began to see pictures in his head. His father. His mother. Nefyn as a child. Joseph had loved them all, in his way. She was in trouble now, though. He could feel it. He'd known she'd send a storm. They'd all known it, but its tempestuousness was breathtaking. There was a darkness when he thought of her. It had always been the other way around – she seemed to know instinctively about his welfare – but now, when he thought of her, there was nothing. He looked up. Looked at his watch. He could hold on no longer. Pulled down his hood, looked up at the sky. Felt the winds sting his face. Took a breath. His whole body was shaking now.

The helicopter sent back the report. White male. Mid-twenties. Probable fisherman in trouble. The Captain took the message, swore, sent a relay around the other watchtowers in case they had noticed anything suspicious. By the time the course of Hamza and Emrys's boat came back, they were already late to dispatch the helicopter to the new coordinates. The Captain stood by the radio, waiting for news. Willing them on. As they flew further out, past the local squall, conditions became calmer, but they were too late. A cargo ship had long since slowed. A dinghy been dispatched. All the helicopter found was a boat, set adrift, empty, save for the body of an elderly gentleman lying dead in its hull.

43

Cove • Kuf • Cildraeth

JOSEPH HAD SAILED BACK to the cove as fast as he could. He was exhausted. His arms aching. His back stiff. The storm had settled and Nefyn lay unconscious in Efa's arms. He had run the boat aground before wading through the water, shouting her name, carrying her in his arms up to the cottage. Efa followed, her heart breaking.

'I tried to stop her,' she said. 'She wouldn't listen.'

'She was buying them time,' he answered. He kicked open the door, the cottage in disarray, ransacked. Joseph looked wordlessly at Efa and carried Nefyn to the chair. He told Efa to light the fire as he pulled Nefyn's wet dress over her head, wrapped her in blankets. Joseph feeling for her pulse. In her wrist, her neck. It was weak and erratic. Efa lit the fire, still in her coat, tried to get some warmth into the place.

'Did you see anything? Did they make it?' Efa asked.

'I don't know,' he muttered, 'I don't know.' Joseph studied Nefyn's face as he rubbed her hands in his.

'Come on, Nefyn . . . please, come on.'

He picked her up, carried her to her bed. Took off his own jumper, slid in under the covers beside her and tried to give her his warmth. Efa came to sit near by, studying them both. Their bodies together out of water. There was nothing to do but wait. Wait for

Nefyn to wake. Wait for news. Wait for the boat to be brought home. Wait for Hamza to come back. Joseph looked at Nefyn. Her breathing shallow. Her skin sullen. A trembling in her neck where her pulse was. He had carried her from the beach before. In the same way. Her eight-year-old body hanging limply as he shouted for his father. His own blood running cold. Her skin tinged with blue, her tongue dumb. He pressed her to him, silently asked her to return to him. Clung to her, childlike, his words gone.

She was drowning now. In air. She could feel it. The dryness stinging her lungs, her skin. She was hanging just below the surface of consciousness. In her mind, she revisited the life she had lived. The path to the cove. The pools where she played with her brother. Her mother's face. This way, she made an act of resurrection. She had half lived before and now, having lived fully with Hamza, she knew that she would not be able to breathe the same again. She thought of the way her mother enfolded her in her arms, the comfort she had felt in her embrace. She thought of the softness of Hamza's stomach, the beauty of his curling hair. She thought of him breathing in the dark. The map they had made. She thought of Efa's love, her gentle worry, and of Emrys's sacrifice. She thought, too, of the shoe-box full of objects that she had placed in Hamza's bag for Hussein. An expression of who she was. The things that she had held dear. The magical smallness of things. Their infinite variety. She lay for a few hours and felt the warmth of Joseph close by her side, and she waited for Efa to fall asleep. When she sensed that she had, her eyes flickered open. Joseph looked up, his eyes exhausted. Her colour was changing. Joseph could see that. She was getting paler. Colder.

'Nefyn?'

'Shsh.' She reached out and placed a finger on his mouth. She smiled at him, took in his face. His russet hair. He kissed her hand.

'I need you to take me to the cove.'

He looked at her incredulously. Shook his head.

'Joseph.'

'I can't.' There was fear in his eyes again.

'Joseph, I need you to be brave.' Nefyn smiled weakly. She raised her arm, tugged at the side of his hair gently. 'Come here.' Her voice was faint as she pulled his head towards her, smiled as she felt his cheek on hers. Then she whispered, 'He was dead, Joseph.'

Joseph turned his eyes in disbelief.

'He was dead when I found him,' she said again.

'No . . .'

She could feel the tremor in his body.

'And I've always known that I could bring someone back.'

Heavy tears fell from Joseph's eyes. He let them fall unimpeded on the blanket that covered them.

'But it's not . . .' he began.

'His love . . . it was enough.' Joseph's vision was blurred; he could not make sense of the words. 'He set me free.' Joseph pulled back, studied her, tried to read her face. 'Can't you see? We set each other free. And I can't live here any more, not like this. I have to go to the sea. I want to. I can't live this half-life.'

Joseph nodded. His tears blinding him.

'You can't leave me.'

'Please, I've felt . . . I've felt enough . . .'

They held each other in silence for a long time. Nefyn feeling the warmth of him under her fingers. He looked up eventually.

'When?' he asked.

She pushed away his tears.

'Now?'

Joseph's eyes widened.

Joseph carried her in the moonlight. She was almost weightless, her slim limbs cold in his. He walked across the stones and set her down on the strandline. She smiled, her eyes drawn to the water. Thirsting. The tide was receding and Nefyn could feel it tugging at the strandline at her feet.

'We're all just a collection of things. Brought together by the sea. Torn apart,' she whispered.

Joseph stood silent, his head falling to his chest like a child's. She rubbed his back.

'Please,' she said. 'Let me go.'

They held each other in their arms. Listened to the sea.

'You're free now, too,' she said.

Joseph nodded. Kissed her head. Held her hand until she pulled away. Their fingers finally releasing each other. Then he watched as she walked slowly into the sea, her eyes fixed on the horizon. As the water pulled at her, she turned back for a moment, smiled fleetingly, the compass glistening at her neck, before disappearing into the dark.

44

Sail ◆ Hwylio ◆ 'abhar

A t Emrys's funeral, Joseph had stood beside Efa like a son. His arm in hers as he walked her back to the car. The church had been full and it had been a comfort to her to know that Emrys was so loved. They had then returned to her house, and Joseph had stayed there, their loneliness binding them together. He had helped her box up Emrys's possessions, his clothes. A few days later, the sailing boat had been returned to them and Joseph had moored her in the harbour, and they had spent many evenings looking out at her in silence.

Efa had thought of staying in the house, but as she began to see the tourists arrive for the summer with their colourful clothes, their own stories, she realized that there was nothing here for her now. She had already given back all the keys to the houses, saying that she had been caretaker too long. It was now time for her to live. She knew she had to start again, whatever that meant. The thought of Nefyn taking her own freedom sustained her when the grief she felt threatened to overwhelm her.

Joseph was to take her to see a small place for sale at the edge of the village, and she waited for him outside the house as the first sunset of summer softened over the bay. She smiled at him as he climbed into the car, and they drove to the small house which over-looked the sea.

Joseph left Efa to look around, and walked along the coastal path towards the cottage. He hadn't slept there since Nefyn had left. It didn't feel like his home any more, but there was something else, too. He had noticed a snaking pattern on the floor, the slight shifting of ground. The squall that Nefyn had summoned seemed to have displaced some rocks in the cove, loosened the soil, tilting the house even further towards the sea. Its angles were strained now, the way it would succumb to the sea inevitable. There was no going back.

As he rounded the coast, it came into view. He stopped for a moment to look, the beauty of its tenuous clinging. He smiled sadly; the buoys, the nets trembling in the breeze. He moved towards the cottage, pushed open the door and took a few steps inside. It was empty. A shell. The stories inside echoing. Joseph felt the now-familiar ache of grief deep inside. It would take time, he knew that.

It was a warm night, the yellowing light illuminating the dust in the air, and his eyes couldn't help but be drawn to the window. To the outside. As he turned to leave, he noticed an envelope on the floor. He moved towards it. Picked it up. A foreign postmark. A slanting hand. It was addressed to Nefyn. He exhaled. Felt its weight in his hands, a burning in his throat and behind his eyes. He carried it out. Made his way down to the cove. The sea was silvery this evening. Whispering. Sounding out its voice, testing its strength. He walked along the beach and stood on the strandline.

Tomorrow morning, he would sail north. Pay his debt. Fulfil his promise. And then? He wasn't sure. He took in the expanse of the sea, felt its vastness settling on him, and for the first time in his life, he was struck by its wondrous beauty.

Acknowledgements • Diolchiadau

Heartfelt thanks to everyone who helped to make this book possible: to my husband for his unwavering support; to my children for being a brilliant source of inspiration and distraction; to my parents and parents-in-law for their kindness through the years. Special thanks also to Anwen Hooson, my agent and friend, for her encouragement and thoughtfulness, and to Alice Youell, who has helmed this book through to publication so skilfully. Thanks also to Richard Anthony, for sharing his military expertise, and Nadine Kaadan, for her cultural guidance. I am also grateful to Nest Llwyd Owen, for granting permission to use her father's poem, and to Professor Peredur Lynch, for sharing his vast knowledge of Gerallt's work. Last but by no means least, my thanks and appreciation to Doubleday, for making me feel so welcome.

Caryl Lewis is a multi-award-winning Welsh novelist, children's writer, playwright and screenwriter. Her breakthrough novel *Martha, Jac a Sianco* (2004) is widely regarded as a modern classic of Welsh literature, and sits on the Welsh curriculum. The film adaptation – with a screenplay by Lewis herself – went on to win six Welsh BAFTAs and the Spirit of the Festival Award at the 2010 Celtic Media Festival. Lewis's other screenwriting work includes BBC/S4C thrillers *Hinterland* and *Hidden*. Lewis is a visiting lecturer in Creative Writing at Cardiff University, and lives with her family on a farm near Aberystwyth. *Drift* is her debut novel in the English language.